Death in a Northern Town 3

Dead Man Walking

By Peter Mckeirnon

ISBN-10: 1517084873

ISBN-13: 1517084875

Cover designed by Wise Owl Imagery – Ian Hewitt

Proof read by Kathryn Begley

Undeadications Page

Katie Watson, Rab Quadir, Kevin Rice, Rebecca Lane, Dicky Crisps, Jo Little, David McDonnell, Marc Mullin, Andy Wilson, Tim Oakes, Anita Blakey, Mike Wharton, Julie Alton, Daniel Greenhalgh, Drew Ridley, Lisa Gerrard, Joshua Dineley, Tracey Reid, Lisa Watson, Stuart Davies, Sam 'Dingo Punch' Jordan, Kris O'Reilly, Joanne Berry, Joanne Edwards, John Williams, Ashleigh Dineley, Lisa Downing, Jane Basnett, Christine Lunt, Kirsty Stoner, Kelly Johnson, Phil Johnson, Si Speddo, Leo Deathe, Stephen Fogg, Judy Neale, Lynn Jay, Emily Wood, Harry Curbishley, Claire M Johnston, Adam Szymura, Mrs Sandra Moose, Tanya Leyshon, Bill Houghton, Lauren Shaw, Neil O'Brien, Paul Williams, Tony Molloy, Rowan Watson, Andy Drummond-Burnett, Katie Davies, Sharon Ludgate, Debby Moss, Kevin Slater, Nykie Brady, Dave Glinos, Benjamin Clarke, Sarah McDowall, Dave Flipp Jones, Tracey Dockerty, Andy Lee, Kevin Bennett, Simon Hallsworth, Sam Jones, Victoria Smith, Mags Dwyer, Andy Savage, Helen Coakley, Leanne Foster, Jen Allford, Nome Clarke, Karl Davies, Jay Parker, Tony Greenhalgh, Niky Perrow, Clare Mann, Dave Tonge, Brandon-Rio Carr, Paula Brownrigg, Jennie Marie Cliffe, Mick Tolley, Susan Watkins, Adrian Stamper, Tashya Melinda Annine Campbell, Isa Brana, David Paul, Paul Smith, Baroness Julia Luxury-Crumpet, Sarah Princess Consuela Banana Hammock Layton, Macklemore, Claire Woods, Rt Hon Richard Ellis, Lauran Shaw, Steven Bradburne, Jason Jay White, Ethan Moore, Andy Coffey, Oldfart Olafson, Robert Mannering, Clare Mannering, Nick Fieldsend, Paul Choat, Johanna Rodriguez, Peter Rodriguez, Charlie Rodriguez, Isabella Rodriguez, Loretta Coppin, Jay Ward, Mike Bignall, Peter Clarke, Andy Coakley, Michael

Pirks OBE, Alby Shellshear, Debbie Sharples, Shirley Mason, Kylie Paul, Paul Prescott, Ian Bethell, Colin Murtagh, Jacqueline Jones.

This novel is dedicated to the memory of Emma Greenhalgh.

Journal Entry 13

My name is John Diant. Tortured father to a missing teenage girl, friend to a retro 1980s music obsessed Scouse smart arse and brother to Runcorn's answer to Chuck Norris, only with less hair and a shitter beard. This is my journal and if you are reading this then hopefully hell is over and order has been restored. If that is the case and zombies are no more then do me a favour and raise a glass so you can join me in a toast.

To the fallen. To everyone we have loved and lost. To the people that touched our lives along the way and to those we will never know. Here's to you. I hope that death has brought you peace.

If of course hell isn't over and you have stumbled across my journal by accident then in all likelihood it means I'm dead or I've misplaced it. If I have lost it then keep an eye out for a dishevelled thirtysomething accompanied by a man carrying a large plastic spoon and a guy with porno mags strapped to his arms. Please be kind and give it back, I promise we won't bite, unlike the rest of this zombie infested town.

A hell of a lot has happened since I last update this journal. I've seen more action than Rambo of late and only now have I found the time and indeed the energy to write everything down. So strap yourselves in because you are in for a very bumpy ride!

"We've got to find her. She can't be out there on her own, she doesn't know what she's doing. She's not thinking straight. I can't lose her I can't!" I cried.

I was again filled with the same panic and fear from a few days earlier; when the zombie outbreak hit and Dave and I went in search of my daughter. Only this time it was different. This time she had more than zombies on her mind. This time she was out for blood, intent on revenge for Jonathon's death. We had made a huge mistake in leaving her with Barry in the hope that sleep would do her good and that she would be kept safe whilst Dave, Butty and I ventured back to my brother's house for supplies. Our plan had backfired, big time! Now she was gone and I had to find her before she did something stupid.

"How long has she been missing?" Butty asked of Barry.

"It's hard to say. I checked on her just after you left this morning, then I opened up the shop and well, it must have been over an hour before I went into the store room again. That's when I noticed she had gone. I ran outside after her but it was impossible to know which direction she had taken. I was hoping maybe she was heading back to the house to meet up with you guys," Barry said sincerely.

"She knows as much as we do and that is that Jonathon's killer drove away towards Weston Point. That's where she'll be going. Knowing our Emily she'll knock down every door on every house until she finds the bastard," Butty said.

"Well then, what the fuck are we waiting for? Let's find some wheels and go look for her. Tool up boys and let's get a move on. We've got about five hours of sunlight and we need to make the most of it. Thanks for the hospitality, Bazza, top notch lar and if I find myself back in the area I'll pop in for a chat, a bag of Space Raiders and a jazz mag but I don't think I'll eat the Raiders first. The last thing I want is pickled onion fingers whilst knocking one out. Later Ace!" Dave said heading for the door.

"It's not your fault Barry please don't punish yourself. This is all my doing. Emily is strong minded, I should have seen this coming. Thanks for all your help and for letting us stay here last night, we won't forget it," I said.

"And thanks for my copy of Splosh, I shall treasure it always and here, take this..." Butty smiled, handing Barry one of his C.B. radios, "Keep in touch. If you have any problems at all you can always get hold of me on this. My handle is Lone Wolf. If for some strange reason I don't answer just ask yourself one question, what would Lone Wolf do?"

Barry took the C.B. radio and gave my brother a look of both bewilderment and confusion. If facial expressions were words then Barry's face was speechless. It's an expression I recognised all too well as over the years I have witnessed it many times. On the faces of family members, friends (when he had some), postmen, door to door salesman, store workers and just about everyone that had come into contact with my brother.

Butty handed me a cricket bat from his stash and taking a crowbar for himself we left BJ & J Owens to begin our search for Emily. We knew where she was likely to be going but not the direction. We had decided it was highly unlikely she would have taken the direct route into Weston Point as it would have involved her passing her uncle's house. She would not have risked being caught and what's more, she would have believed Jonathon's body to still be tied to a lamp post, not knowing that Dave had moved him inside the house. She wouldn't put herself through the ordeal of seeing him like that.

No, she would have chosen a different route, probably cutting through the back roads, taking her behind her Uncle's house and into Weston Point that way.

"It's what I would do and over the years I've tried to teach our Emily everything I know," Butty concluded.

That was good enough for me so that's where we headed only first we needed transport and further along the street was a small block of flats with secure, undercover parking. It was the logical place to look and Dave was a good 100 yards ahead of us by the time we left the shop, stopping only to search the bodies of the dead for any cigarettes they may have and thwarting the occasional attacking zombie with his Battle Paddle. The area was still relatively zombie free apart from a few stragglers that is. The lure of The Pavilions and the smell from the many corpses in the road was keeping the majority of the deaders away.

"What are you thinking brother?" I asked, hoping for a reply that would ease my tired and worried mind.

"I'm thinking we need to get Dave some nicotine patches to help him quit smoking. If he carries on at this rate there'll soon be more stubbed out cigarette butts than corpses in this town. What was he like in work? I mean, I take it he wasn't allowed to smoke whilst making mayonnaise?" Butty asked.

"Well it would take him five minutes to prepare a batch of mayo and then another five minutes for it to cook. So he would be smoking whilst the machinery mixed all the ingredients together. Then he'd come back, bring me a sample of the disgusting gloop to test then bugger off for another fag before coming back for the results. So that's a fag every five minutes and Dave worked eight hour shifts with an hour lunch break and he could smoke even more during that time. He could probably get through over one hundred smokes in an eight hour shift," I replied.

"How the hell is he still alive? I mean, I like a cigarette every now and again but he takes it to another level." Butty asked with amazement.

How Dave is alive is a question I've asked myself many times over the years. I remember him going to the doctors with a chest infection. Dave was getting a little concerned that his excessive smoking was starting to impact his health so the docs did a lung capacity test and the results came back saying he was perfectly healthy and his lungs were fine. He celebrated by going on a ciggie run to France, bringing back thousands of cartons of fags! The man is a smoking machine!

We arrived at the entrance to the car park which was secured by large steel garage doors. There we found Dave waiting for us, leaning against the wall casually smoking a tab.

"That was quite a profitable little jaunt. 6 packets of ciggies I found in the pockets of the dead. That's the great thing about this town. Every other person smokes. Here you go Butty lad suck on one of these," he said, throwing a cigarette to my brother. "I'll tell you what though, I found a couple of those vapour cigarette thingummyjigs. You know the type, the ones that look like Dr fucking Who's sonic screwdriver. It's a good job the zombies came before those things got really popular or bifters could be sparse lad. Why would you smoke one of those things anyway? If you're gonna quit then quit. Don't puff on something that looks like a nose hair trimmer because you think it makes you look cool. It doesn't, it makes you look like a cu…"

Cutting Dave off mid rant was a horrific groan, echoing through the interior of the undercover car park. I peeked through the metal barred window to see a young women wearing a dark blue business suit with a white blouse. She had blood dried around her mouth, neck and blouse and in her right hand she dragged behind her a small travel suitcase. She was shuffling without direction with one ankle twisted, pulling along a broken foot tucked inside a broken high heeled shoe.

"Look at the state of this," Dave said, "dressed up like some high powered business women. I hate yuppies like this, always chasing the fucking coin and what's the deal with the suitcase? They all drag those silly little suitcases with the massive handles around don't they? Suppose it makes them look important like they always have somewhere they need to be. A tenner says there's nothing inside but a make-up bag and a copy of Take a Break."

"Can you see any other zombies in the car park?" Butty asked, unzipping his holdall and rooting through the contents before retrieving a very large crowbar.

I looked again through the barred window. The winter sunlight partially lit the inside of the car park and from what I could see, the zombie business woman was the only one in there. Beyond her were several parked cars. I turned to my brother and shook my head, informing that no other zombies were visible.

Butty forced a crowbar underneath the metal shutters then he began pulling and tugging, loosening the steel garage door from its frame. In no time at all he had forced a gap big enough for us to crawl through.

"Are you coming then or are you going to stay here holding your dicks all day? I'll go first and dispose of the zombie," Butty informed.

"No chance Ace, I saw her first. I'm gonna ram that suitcase so far down her throat she'll need a rectal examination to open it. Hold this Johnny boy..." Dave grinned, handing me his Battle Paddle before crawling through the gap in the garage door.

Butty and I followed him into the garage then watched as without a weapon and whilst smoking a cigarette Dave casually approached the zombie, like it was the most natural thing in the world. His fleshy scent launched the deader into a frenzy and it began moving towards him, drooling and gnashing its teeth. Now if you can remember, Dave was the only one of us not wearing zombie limb links as he didn't want to ruin his retro threads.

"I always have this effect on the birds," he smirked, "alright calm down girl you'll ladder your tights if you don't control yourself!"

The zombie girl made a grab for Dave who expertly dodged her advances and positioned himself behind her. Before she had figured out where her intended meal had moved to, he grabbed the suitcase out of her hand and began smashing it hard into her face until she was no more. His final face smash shattered the suitcase and out of it fell a make-up bag and a copy of Hello Magazine.

"You owe us both a tenner. Take a Break you said, that's Hello Magazine," I informed smugly.

"Ah fuck, it was a pretty good guess though," Dave replied.

Dave searched the dead zombie's pockets, finding a purse and inside it a £20 note.

"Here you go you pair of bastards," he said, ripping the note in two and giving us half each, "Don't spend it all at once."

Then we heard more groaning, only this time the sound was fuller and louder. Out of the shadows at the far end of the car park shuffled seven zombies.

"I'm sure you need bloody glasses!" Butty yelled at me before running at the lead zombie, smashing it hard in the forehead with his crowbar.

Before the zombie had hit the ground another closed in on my brother, leaning in to chomp on his neck. Butty reached out with his porno magazine covered forearm and placed it in the deader's mouth.

With the zombie chewing on the heavily laminated copy of 'Juicy Whoppers', Butty hammered his crowbar repeatedly into the top of his attackers head.

"Some help would be appreciated boys!" he yelled.

With two zombies down there were still five to contend with and they were a rotting assembly of one female and four males. All wearing business suits.

I passed Dave his Battle Paddle. He ran forward a few steps then launched the giant mayonnaise stirring instrument through the air towards the oncoming undead. What a shot it was or as Dave so elegantly put it… "His fucking head came off!"

Like a javelin athlete of Olympic ability (only with sunglasses on and tab hanging out of his mouth), Dave had propelled his Battle Paddle towards the oncoming gathering of flesh eaters with astounding precision (or sheer luck as I suspected). The unconventional weapon hit one of the male zombies in the neck, slicing through tissue and bone removing its rotting head clean from its body. The fire damaged paddle was now jagged and spear like in its appearance and it cut through the zombie like a knife through butter.

"Fluke!" Butty shouted, drilling his crowbar into the head of another approaching zombie.

Three zombies to go and as I had so far stood by and watched Dave and Butty dispose of the advancing undead, the pressure was building for me to join in and do my bit for the team. With cricket bat in hand I joined the zombie bashing party and pelted the woman in the face as hard as I could. Broken teeth and dark thickening blood flew through the air as the thwack from the bat broke her jaw which now hung loosely, barely attached to her face. A cold shiver ran down my spine and the impact of the blow reverberated through my body.

I've said it before and no doubt I'll say it again but killing zombies, for me, does not come easy. The sinking feeling in the pit of my stomach, the retching motion that follows and despair that swallows me upon killing the undead has not eased over the past few days. Maybe it's just me as the company I'm keeping seems to be enjoying it!

The zombie business woman shuffled towards me, her jaw swinging below her bloodied nose; the threads of tissue and skin holding it in place loosened more with every step. I swung the bat once more with as much strength as I could muster and watched as her head cracked open on impact and her jaw broke away from her mouth.

Then I puked and in case any of you were wondering, spam looks almost the same coming out as it does going in!

By the time I had finished vomiting I looked up to see Butty and Dave standing victorious over the two remaining zombies puffing their chests out and proudly displaying their killing weapons like a pair of apocalyptic peacocks.

"You're still struggling with this zombie killing aren't you ace?" Dave rightly observed.

"I have told you before little brother, they are not people anymore. Nothing of what made them human remains. They feel nothing and desire only to feed, you need to remember that John," Butty barked, pointing his finger at me like a school teacher on a power trip.

"Oh I remember alright but it's easier said than done when you're faced with the prospect of twatting a dead person in the face with a cricket bat. I wouldn't find it so difficult if they didn't look like us," I explained.

"You'll get over it, you're gonna have to if we're going to find Emily because between now and when we find her, and we will find her, there's going to be a hell of a lot more dead people to kill," Butty replied.

"That's right kidda and look on the bright side, in a few days these dead bastards won't look as fresh as they do now. They will look barely human at all apart from the clothes on their backs. I reckon you'll find it a lot easier in a few days," Dave confidently informed.

I wasn't so sure.

"Now then which one will it be?" Butty said, referring to the many parked cars that surrounded us.

He lent over a fallen zombie and began searching through his pockets before retrieving a set of car keys. He pressed the key fob and the lights flashed and doors unlocked on a large top of the range Land Rover, very similar to the vehicle Dave had dismissed outside the Mayonnaise factory in favour of the Ford Thunderbird. It wasn't until Butty and I were inside the Land Rover that we realised Dave had not followed and was instead circling an old brown Volvo Estate like it was a Jaguar F-Type.

Dave reached into his pocket, retrieved a 2 pence piece and placed it into the lock of the Volvo's door, opening it with very little struggle. Once inside he found a spare set of keys in the glove compartment and revved the engine joyfully a few times before pulling up in front of us, winding down his window.

"If you think I'm travelling in that thing when there's vintage wheels like this classic Volvo available, you can think again. They don't make them like this anymore lar. It might be a bit boxy but it's sturdy and well built, great MPG and of course the icing on the cake, it has a fucking tape player! Also, look what I found in the glove compartment..." Dave said excitedly, lifting his hands in the air to reveal he was wearing brown leather driving gloves.

"How cool do I look wearing these bad boys? In fact, there's no need to respond because I already know the answer. I feel like James fucking Bond, only cool 1980s Roger Moore James bond, not your pouting, trunk wearing, moody arse Daniel Craig James Bond. Roger's eyebrows alone have more acting talent than Danny Craig has in his entire body. Also look at this. Whoever this car belongs to had some great taste in music. I was gonna blast out some Ultravox but I've got the Best of Tom Jones here. What a perfect soundtrack for our mission to find Emily," he continued.

Dave slotted a cassette into the Volvo's tape player and Kiss by Tom Jones began to play. He sparked up a cigarette and said…

"The name's Dave, 80s Dave. License to be Ace!"

Then he drove out of the car park.

Drink Till They Die

"Tony? The Karaoke is fired up and I thought we could maybe have a go at singing a duet. Me and little Sophie have been singing all night and we don't want you to miss out on the fun! Maybe a bit of 'Don't Go breaking My Heart' by Elton John and Kiki Dee. Don't worry I don't mind being Kiki but I'll have to borrow that leopard print fur coat of yours to get into character. If you don't fancy singing that one we could always go for a bit of 'Real Dead Ringer For Love' by Meatloaf and Cher. You can be Cher though as I reckon you've got better legs than me. Tony? Are you still sleeping? You've been gone for hours mate. Tony?"

It was early morning and Nick had not seen Tony since the previous evening when the Terrorvision front man had gone to find an empty apartment to rest in. After surviving a plane crash and being attacked by zombies he was beat but Nick was missing his new friend and wanted somebody to share a drink with.

Nick walked out on to the hallway – His long black hair hanging in front of his face and a half empty bottle of Jack Daniels in his hand. He turned and looked through the open door at Sophie. She was dancing and singing along with microphone in hand, warbling to a sickly sweet pop song. On the couch was baby Gaby, laughing hysterically at her big sister's antics. Nick smiled and considered how resilient children can be. A little over two days had passed since their father had been eaten alive by zombie ducks and geese and their mother, from what Sophie had told him, was very sick and he held no doubt that she too would now be dead. Yet there was Sophie, dancing and singing like she hadn't a care in the world. Though he had only known them a short time, a strong bond had formed and he deeply cared for the children. They were his only light in a world filled with darkness. Apart from his new apocalypse running buddy, Tony, of course.

He walked down the stairwell of Churchill Mansions to the hallway below and entered through the open doorway of the closest apartment. He knew this home well. Before the outbreak it had belonged to Billy, an old man and good friend of Nick's grandmother but he knew him better as Trust No One, founding member of Aliens of Runcorn Spotters Elite or A.R.S.E. as it was better known.

An ex-military man, Trust No One was obsessed with aliens and claimed to have been abducted and experimented on many times, referring to a scar on his lower abdomen to where they had removed and then later replaced all of his internal organs. As a child Nick was fascinated by this story and believed every word. That is until he had his appendix removed aged thirteen and received a scar exactly the same. Still, he enjoyed the old man's company and loved nothing more than to listen to crazy tales about alien life forms, the imminent invasion of our planet and the plans that he and other A.R.S.E members had in place for the end of the world. It pained Nick to have had to kill him. But like the rest of the apartment block, including his beloved Grandmother, he had become the undead and every last one had to die in order for him to secure the building.

Just as he was moving to leave the apartment, droplets of glistening blood on the carpet leading to the living room window caught his eye.

The closer he got to the blood the more of it he saw. Red droplets turned into a pool of sticky plasma soaked into the old dirty carpet. It was fresh and there was more dripping down the wall below the window. He ran to the window and opened it quickly looking to the ground below.

Amongst the many zombie corpses surrounding the apartment block lay Tony; his body twisted and bloodied from the fall.

Nick strained his tired eyes and looked closely at the body. Tony had been ripped open across his stomach, a wound that did not look to have been caused by the fall. He quickly turned away from the window and looked again to the blood stains in the apartment. He hadn't noticed at first but there were bloodied footprints imprinted in the carpet leading to the apartment door.

He wasn't alone.

"Fuck!" Nick exclaimed before running out of the doorway and up the stairwell to his apartment.

When he arrived at his apartment door, the same sickly pop song could be heard from his karaoke machine only it wasn't Sophie that was singing. It was a deep dull voice that sounded like it belonged to a man of some stature. He tightened his grip on his bottle of Jack Daniels and forcefully opened the door, bursting into his apartment.

There he saw in front of him a large heavy set man singing into a microphone held closely to his mouth. His other arm was wrapped around Sophie tightly with his hand smothering her petrified face. On the couch sat on old thin women with short grey hair and skin like cracked leather. In one arm she cradled a sleeping Gaby and in her other she held a decapitated hand which she was bringing down slowly towards the infant's face.

"What the hell are you doing?" Nick questioned sharply.

"So nice of you to join us. I was wandering how long it would take for you to realise that you were not alone in this building. My name is Blanche, I live in apartment thirteen and that handsome fine specimen of a man over there is my son, Walter. I guess you were not as thorough as you thought when you secured the building huh? I was an acquaintance of your Grandmother's. I wouldn't go as far as to say we were friends because if truth be told I disliked the old bitch. She was always so, nice to everyone, I just couldn't stand to be around her. She loved you though and the bitch talked about you all the time. She was always telling everyone how kind you are and how you always made time to visit and look after her. Deluded old fool but I digress... You're arrival here is perfect. You can watch as I finally get to prove my theory," she said.

"And what theory is that? That you're both a pair of crazy bastards that killed my friend? I don't think that's a theory, that's the truth if you ask me!" Nick snarled.

"My theory, you drunken piece of shit, is the younger you are when you become infected, the quicker it takes for you to turn into a zombie. Which means the older you are, the longer it will take for you to die. Take a seat whilst I show you..." she said, moving the decapitated hand closer to Gaby's face.

"You touch her and I swear to God I'm going to fuck you up!" Nick yelled, shaking with anger.

"What are these girls to you anyway? They are not yours, you are not their father. Walter and I watched as you saved them from the ducks outside but why? Why would you risk your life to save theirs? To save your soul perhaps? Because you've led a worthless life, wasted on drink and the occasional money begging visit to your granny to see you through to your next government hand out? Look at the state of you. You're nothing but a chancer, a loser with nobody to love and nobody left to love you. We've been watching you since the outbreak Nick. The only person you had in the world turned into a zombie and you killed her. You're scum and these girls will be better dead than living with you!" Blanche responded, her thin lips stretching into an evil smile.

"Wrong!" Nick replied purposefully.

Walter pushed Sophie to the ground and started to move towards Nick with determination, growling with his mouth wide open as his moved. Nick flipped the Jack Daniels bottle so that he was holding the base then removing its lid he ran at Walter, thrusting the neck of the liquor bottle down into the big guy's throat.

"My boy! What have you done to my boy?" Blanche screamed, rising to her feet with Gaby in her embrace.

Walter had fallen to his knees. With his neck tilted back he clawed at his mouth trying desperately to remove the bottle from his throat, coughing and spluttering Jack Daniels as he drowned from the constant liquid pouring into his mouth.

Using the palm of his hand Nick pushed hard on the base of the bottle, driving it deeper into Walter's throat. He pushed it so deep that the outline of the bottle was visible through the skin of his neck.

With his last breath Walter reached out to his mother before collapsing face down onto the floor. Consumed with despair Blanche screamed then brought the zombie hand inches from Gaby's face, a dirty jagged finger nail ready to scrape across her forehead.

Quickly Sophie wrapped her arms around Blanche's thin, vain covered legs and bit deep into her calf. The old women shrieked in pain, releasing her grip on the mutilated zombie hand.

Nick rushed towards Blanche and placing a hand around her dried out leathery neck he began to squeeze causing her cataract loaded eyes to bulge from the pressure.

"Take your sister and go to the bedroom Sophie," he instructed and she did so without question, "Now then, that theory of yours. Let's put it to the test shall we?"

He picked up the zombie limb with his free hand and dragged Blanche by her neck out onto the balcony of the apartment, pushing her against the railings, bending her upper body backwards over the edge of the building.

"So the young turn quickly do they? Then you should be in for a long and painful transformation!" Nick snarled, scratching her face with a rotting finger from the mutilated hand.

"It… was… me…" Blanche croaked.

"What did you say?" Nick questioned, loosening his grip slightly so that she could speak.

"Your... grandmother. I gave her the... infection. I gave it to all of them. I infected everyone. They all deserved it..." she rasped.

Unable to control his anger Nick gripped her neck tightly and began to push, again bending her upper body backwards over the balcony railing.

Crack!

Her face contorted with pain as the frail bones in her back began to break.

Crunch!

The noise of her spine snapping only enraged Nick more and he pushed his hand deep into her throat, snapping her neck backwards, forcing her broken body over the balcony and down to the road below.

He moved away from the edge of the balcony and slowly walked back into the apartment, taking a moment to compose himself before entering the bedroom where Sophie sat nursing her sleeping sister.

"I messed up. I thought I'd checked every apartment but I..." he started, struggling to find words.

"Is your new friend dead? He is isn't he?" Sophie asked,

"Yes," came Nick's solemn reply.

"I don't like it here. Bad things happen. Teddy doesn't like it either, he says he wants to leave," she continued.

"I don't think I like it anymore either and if Teddy says he wants to leave then we leave. I'll get a few things together, you look after your sister for me," he smiled before leaving the bedroom, closing the door behind him.

Nick sat down heavily onto the couch and reflected on what had just happened. Killing that evil women and her son barely felt real but he was sure of one thing and that was they deserved it. What the evil old women was about to do to Gaby and the revelation that she had spread the zombie infection within Churchill Mansions was enough to justify his actions.

He looked at the woman's son lying dead in front of him. The big guy's head lay in a pool of blood and alcohol and next to him the karaoke system which still played horrible pop music. The smell of bourbon filling the room made Nick very thirsty. He turned off the karaoke machine and entered the kitchen, taking another bottle of Jack Daniels from his well-stocked supplies.

Opening the bottle and bringing it to his lips he heard the sound of Sophie talking in the bedroom, whispering to her baby sister. Moving the bottle away from his mouth he re-entered the living room and gently pressed his ear against the bedroom door.

"We'll be OK Gaby. Mummy and Daddy have gone to heaven but we've got Uncle Nick now. Uncle Nick is funny but he drinks too much. I think I'll ask Teddy to talk to him and get him to stop. We don't like it do we Teddy..."

Nick took himself back out onto the balcony and lent against the railing with the bottle of liquor in his hands. The sound of groaning could be heard from the road and he looked down to see the twisted and torn body of Blanche on the ground below, her badly damaged head moving slowly, shifting from side to side.

"Goodbye old friend," he said to his bottle of Jack before dropping it over the balcony.

The bottle fell swiftly, gathering pace before connecting with Blanche' head, dispersing blood, brain, glass and liquor across the road.

Suddenly it became darker. The street lights below that had been providing extra illumination to the dark winter morning had shut off. He looked into the apartment and the lights had gone off also. The power going out reminded him of his conversations with Trust No One and how the old man had informed him this would happen when the aliens invaded.

"When the greys come, the first thing they'll do is cut off our power supply. That's how they'll get us you see. We'll be easy pickings and practically defenceless against their superior technology. But I have a plan, well a friend really. Lone Wolf is his name. He's a fellow Alien Spotter and all round apocalypse expert. When the shit goes down, I'll be heading to his place. He's got weapons, food supplies, power generators… It will be the safest place in Runcorn let me tell you. Now us Spotters don't usually share personal details like our addresses but me and Lone Wolf go way back. Hey, if anything happens to me and you need somewhere to go, there's a bug out bag hidden behind false panelling in my kitchen cupboard. Everything you need is in there. Just remember to tell Lone Wolf that Trust No One sent you, he'll see you right…"

Nick ran out onto the hallway and down into Trust No One's apartment, opening the kitchen cupboards then removing the panelling from the back to reveal a secret compartment containing a large duffle bag. It was full of apocalyptic supplies. Water canisters, med kits, a helmet covered in tin foil to block aliens attempting to read your mind, knives, a baseball bat and crowbars and last but not least was a hand drawn map of Runcorn showing the way from Churchill Mansions to Lone Wolf's house.

Journal Entry 14

It can be a difficult thing trying to figure out the mind of a teenage girl. Believe me I know and I have been on the receiving end of the dreaded glare, the feared huff, the sinister sigh and the menacing strop on many an occasion. But in Zombie Land things are a little different because now when I ask myself 'What would Emily Do?' I know that she's asking herself 'What would Uncle Butty do?' Luckily for me, I had the crazy bastard next to me, tutting and swearing under his breath as we drove slowly behind 80's Dave in his boxy old Volvo Estate.

We had left Balfour Street and turned on to Picow Farm Road. It was a long road containing both houses and industrial units that ran adjacent to Weston Point. All we needed was to drive far enough along so we could turn left into the housing estate and come up behind my brother's house. I tried to take in as much of our surroundings as possible, hoping to find a sign that Emily had been this way but there was nothing. Only the aftermath of apocalyptic chaos.

A burnt out car that had mounted the curb was the first thing that greeted us. The vehicle was black and blistered and glass from every window lay shattered on the ground. Crawling out of the front passenger door was a zombie, so badly burnt it resembled a stick of Peperami only with arms and legs. With no hair, no clothes and barely any skin, the zombie's upper torso rested on top of sharp fragments of glass; its legs trapped inside the car by a tangled seatbelt.

A large rat sat directly in front of the car, nibbling at the remains of a dead pigeon. The burnt zombie was clawing at the road in a desperate attempt to break free from the vehicle and eat the rodent; its skinless mouth exposed charred blackened teeth gnashing together. The rat occasionally lifted its head out of the pigeon's carcass, glanced at the zombie then returned to its meal. The rodent knew that the barbecued deader was not a threat.

On the other side of the road there was a row of bungalows, several with their doors open and many with boxes of belongings left on their front lawns. Others had half boarded up windows and one bungalow had an elderly couple dead in the doorway. Both with stab wounds through their chests but no damage was visible to their heads. They had been the victim of looters. Poor bastards. The end of the world seems to favour those without morals, principles and decency. Just like the guy that murdered Jonathon.

The only other things that remained were shufflers, wondering aimlessly, sporadically placed up and down the road. They were not a threat, not whilst we were in our vehicles, although 80s Dave was doing his best to get their attention; driving along casually smoking a cigarette, one arm leaning out of his open window and 'It's Not Unusual' by Tom Jones pumping out of the Volvo's stereo.

"Do you know what I miss about life before the apocalypse?" Butty said.

"Now let me see. You hate people so that can't be it. You always moaned how crap television is calling it government controlled drivel; drip feeding the masses visual sedatives like X Factor, Big Brother, endless cooking programmes and bilge such as Cash in the Attic and Extreme Makeover so we all stay asleep and ignorant to the atrocities being committed by world leaders, so it can't be that. You often state that there hasn't been a good movie released since

29

Escape from New York and the internet is filled with nothing but cat videos and porn so it can't be either of those. Well you've got me stumped so tell me, what is it you miss?" I replied.

"Birds. The sky is completely empty now. Sometimes I'd climb out of the window in my attic and relax on the roof just looking up at the sky, watching as large groups of starlings whizzed past, diving up and down and circling the Runcorn Bridge. It always amazed me how they kept formation and never flew into each other. Now of course instead of looking up I just look down. The streets and roads are littered with them," said Butty sadly as the Land Rover jolted over feathered corpses.

"Why do you think this happened to them?" I asked.

"Remember me telling you I was tracking the outbreak as it headed across Europe from Russia? There were unconfirmed reports of birds falling from the skies from the start. There was a complete media blackout on this of course as world leaders tried to keep everything under wraps in the hope they could contain it. Videos of birds falling to their death appeared on YouTube. That is if you were lucky enough to see them before the Nazis at Google took them down. I saw them though. Europe quickly became a feathery graveyard," Butty told.

"So that's it then, no birds? Every last one of them is dead?" I asked.

"Not quite. I still haven't told you about the ducks have I? FUCK ME!" my brother yelled.

Butty's expletive outburst was due to 80s Dave slamming on the brakes causing us to almost smash into the rear of his Volvo Estate. Before we had a chance to scream at our retro friend for his terrible driving, further on in the road heading straight for us, was a large coach and it was on fire!

"Put the fucker in reverse!" Dave shouted.

Butty obliged and we, with Dave in front, reversed backwards quickly as the flaming vehicle drew closer and closer. I couldn't take my eyes off the coach and watched as its windows burst from the heat of the fire and glass dispersed on to the road.

Out of the broken windows I saw blistered arms reaching out, covered in flames.

"Jump!" Butty yelled at me.

"You fucking jump!" I replied.

"Do it! I'll be right behind you!" he growled.

Reluctantly, I opened the car door and jumped, only I was still wearing my seatbelt and almost split myself in two! Butty looked at me disapprovingly and shook his head as I was propelled back into my seat. Even with an oncoming fireball heading his way he still found time to make me feel like a Muppet.

Releasing the seatbelt, I tumbled out of the Land Rover and rolled towards the pavement. I brought my head up to see Dave reverse past, one hand on the wheel and the other over the back of the driver's seat, his body turned to the side so that he could see where he was driving. Then the fire ball of a coach whizzed past. The fiery arms that I had noticed early had grown in numbers and the interior appeared loaded with passengers engulfed with flames.

Butty turned the Land Rover into the driveway of one of the bungalows and parked up, knocking through a small brick garden wall to do so. Dave followed suit only his reverse parking was superb, pulling into the driveway of the bungalow next to Butty.

The coach continued to hurtle along the road until it veered to the right, hit the curb and flipped onto its side sending it skidding before coming to a halt and then finally exploding, sending bodies flying through the air.

Butty looked on from his car window whilst Dave stepped out of the Volvo and removed his sunglasses to watch as badly burnt bodies were launched in every direction. It was like watching a kid witnessing the greatest firework display of all time. His eyes were filled with wonder and I swear I could hear him say "Ooh!" and "Ah!" as each blistered corpse shot skyward.

As Dave and my brother enjoyed the entertainment I could hear groans behind me. A couple of shufflers had my scent in their decaying nostrils and were heading my way. Having left the cricket bat in the car, I ran to the broken wall Butty had destroyed and grabbed a couple of bricks for weapons then walked towards the oncoming rotters. My stomach once again churned and warm saliva filled my mouth but there was no time to be sick, I had to do what needed to be done.

I placed one brick on the ground and smashed the other into the forehead of the closest zombie, putting an end to the smelly bastard.

BOOM!

The coach exploded for a second time and Dave began to applaud accompanied with enthusiastic cheers of "More!" and "Bravo!" The explosion startled me so much that I lost my footing and tripped over the brick I had placed on the ground, falling backwards on my arse with a zombie closing in.

Like a gift from God (if he/she was a sick and twisted shit bag) a smouldering decapitated arm fell from the heavens and landed in my lap. The zombie was closing in and with no time to reach for the brick, I grabbed the decapitated arm in a hand shake and whacked the deader across the head, causing it to stagger sideways momentarily before resuming its pursuit. I whacked it across the head again, this time knocking it to the ground. With my spare hand I retrieved the brick and continually pounded it into the zombies face until it was dead.

I stood there for a few seconds, glaring at the pulp of broken face whilst I caught my breath. Man my heart was beating so fast I could see it pounding out of my chest. Then I realised I was still shaking hands with the mutilated arm of a dead person. A shiver took over my whole body and I retched and squirmed in disgust. I released my grip but the dead hand stayed attached to my palm which was now beginning to burn. I hadn't noticed before but the arm was smouldering from the coach fire. Maybe it was adrenaline but my brain had not registered the heat and I had felt no pain at first. But now? Fuck me my hand felt like it was being baked in an oven.

I yanked the blistered limb free and threw it to the ground. But I could still feel something stuck to my hand. It was skin. Red sticky flesh had slithered free from the burnt appendage and attached itself to my hand which now looked like it had been dipped in rhubarb and custard.

I climbed over the broken wall and began wiping my hand manically into the frost coated grass. The cool frozen blades not only helped to remove the sticky burnt skin from my hand but also ease the pain. Only now the smell of burning flesh was in my nostrils and I curled up my noise in disgust, making me look like a demented rabbit.

"What's up with your face? You look like someone that's taken a shit then ran out of toilet paper with one wipe to go and had to walk around with a shitty arse all day. You're missing the entertainment over here, John," Dave said, referring to the human fire work display.

My hand now as clean as it was going to get and with the burning sensation eased, I marched past Dave towards my brother and opened the driver's door.

"Butty! Why the hell did you make me jump from a moving car if you were then just going to park the fucking thing? You could have killed me!" I moaned.

"Stop moaning you're alright aren't you? I was going to jump too but then I realised I could just park up in this driveway. You should be made up. I've always wanted to play stuntman and jump from a moving vehicle. Count yourself lucky," Butty replied.

"Lucky? I've just tumbled out of a moving car, narrowly missed being ran over by a motorised fire ball then had to fend off two attacking zombies with a brick and a barbequed arm! And you think I should count myself lucky?" I fumed.

"If there was ever a definition of lucky, I'd say you're it Ace. I mean look at the kip of you, you're a jibbering wreck. You get your tits in a twist over anything, you puke every time you kill a zombie, you're always moaning about your back and you squirm whenever mayonnaise is mentioned. The fact you are still alive is quite remarkable if you ask me. That makes you pretty fucking lucky kid," Dave offered, not moving his eyes from the coach crash. "Come on then ladies let's give this coach a closer inspection. The blaze is quietening down and it looks like the firework display is over, which is a shame. It was like midnight on an apocalyptic New Year's Eve. I had the end of Tchaikovsky's 1812 Overture going through my head whilst body parts exploding into the sky. Der der der der der der der der der LEGS, der der der der der der der der der der der HEAD, der der der der der der der der der der FEET! Fucking magical!"

Dave threw the remains of a cigarette to the grass and took a few steps towards the crash. Then we heard motorbikes approaching accompanied by cheers and laughter.

"Inside the bungalow now!" Butty instructed.

We ran through the open doorway of the nearest bungalow and crouched beneath the living room window. My brother reached into his pocket and retrieved a small compact mirror.

"I don't think this is the right time for checking your appearance Ace but if it helps, you're still an ugly bastard," Dave smiled.

Butty gave Dave the 'Shut the fuck up' look and he obliged, sensing for once that this might not be the best time for piss taking.

The rumble from the motorbikes quickly became deafening and it was evident that whoever they were, they were now directly outside. As quickly as the noise had erupted it decreased as each motorbike came to halt and only the cheers and laughter remained.

35

Butty positioned himself to the side of the window, tilting his compact mirror so he could see how many had gathered outside.

"Four motorbikes, four men, one women. All heavily armed. Baseball bats, knives, tools... the works," he whispered.

We sat quietly, listening to the survivors outside talking amongst themselves.

"Can you believe this shit? This is so cool man, there are bodies everywhere. The fucking thing exploded!"

"So who won?"

"Billy was closest,"

"Fuck you Billy, I was closest, I won. I won the bet!"

"No way, you weren't even close. You said it wouldn't make it past the skip yard,"

"Did not."

"Did so!"

"Hey hey put your handbags away. Billy, you won the bet, go and claim your prize. Don't even think about objecting Johno or I'll rip your fucking head off and feed it to the next zombie we see! Go on then Billy, what's it going to be? Beak or pills?"

"Beak man, I can't ride on a trip."

"Here, take your prize. What next guys? There is plenty of daylight and plenty of drugs, let's see how much more fun we can have before we head back!"

Cheers of agreement and the revving of motorbike engines followed before the rumbling disappeared into the distance. Dave moved to light a cigarette but my brother signalled for him to keep still. Something Butty was witnessing in his compact mirror had him on edge. Then after a short while the revving and rumbling of another motorbike riding into the distance was heard.

"Ok we can move now," Butty said with relief.

"What did you see?" I asked.

"Trouble. The sort of trouble we don't want any part of right now. Not with all the other shit we've got going on. The bloke that seemed to be running things stayed a little longer than the others. Something caught his eye. Your cigarette Dave, the one you threw away. He saw it smoking on the grass then he glanced towards both cars and I swear before he left, he looked right at this mirror and winked at me. Winked!" An angry Butty explained.

"Come on let's go, just in case they come back. We've wasted too much time already, Emily could be anywhere by now," I interjected.

Leaving the bungalow we took another look at the fiery coach. Zombies, blistered and burnt crawled out of the wreckage, slowly making their way towards us.

"Top Butty survival tip for you John. Never set fire to a zombie. They don't give a shit and just keep on coming. I mean eventually the fire will burn through to their brain and kill them but they can do a lot of damage before that happens. Imagine a marching horde of zombies, maybe a hundred or so and they are all on fire. I'm talking an army of undead fireballs. They would light up everything they touched and Runcorn would burn. Nope, setting fire to a zombie is never a good idea. Unless of course, destroying everything is your intention. Then there is no better way." Butty considered, talking more to himself rather than to me.

Dave pulled out of the driveway and we followed, continuing a little further along Picow Farm Road before turning left into Weston Point. The roads here are long and narrow with terraced houses running along either side. Cars abandoned and the remains of the dead littered the streets. Then of course there were zombies. More of them than before which was leading me to believe that the Human vs. Dead war that had been raging at The Pavilions was over and the dead had won.

Where the hell was my daughter?

Emily

"Straight ahead will take me to Uncle Butty's house but what if they are still there? If I turn right then I can come up behind my uncle's house and start looking for him there. Turn left and I can cut through Runcorn Hill, coming out ahead of the house. Then I can follow in the direction the bastard drove away. Come on Emily make up your freakin' mind!"

Emily stood in the road, a hammer in hand and a display of dead zombies surrounding her. It had been close to an hour since she gave Barry the slip, sneaking out of his newsagents to find the man that killed Jonathon, but she hadn't made it very far. Consumed by hate she was struggling to find focus. Unable to decide on a direction to take she had instead stayed still, slaying any zombie that had attacked.

Then she heard a voice in the distance and her mind became clear.

"Like I said Ace, Phil Collins, although a massive tool, is responsible for reinventing Genesis and making their sound more accessible. Land of Confusion, Invisible Touch, Domino, Mama... all classic tracks lar and completely blow the socks off any of the bollocks you hear today. When Collins moved to lead vocals it took them to another level and far removed them from their experimental days with Peter Gabriel. Now Peter Gabriel is a different kind of lunatic all together. He went from wearing massive fuck off animal heads in the 70's to whacking himself with a virtual sledgehammer in the 80s. Steam, Sledgehammer and the beautiful Don't Give up with Kate Bush are all time classics kid. Now Kate Bush, she is on a different planet all together. I mean, what the fuck is Babooshka all about?"

"You're so stuck in the past Dave. There has been plenty of decent music released since the 80s. You should broaden your horizons. Spread your musical wings and appreciate something a little more modern."

"More modern my arse! I suppose you'd have me listening to Pharrell Williams or some other modern day shite. Well you can jog on if you think I'm listening to him. What is it he sings? Clap along if you feel like a home without a roof? I have two problems with that line. One, homes can't feel as they are non-living things and two, even if they could feel I doubt they'd be happy without a roof kid. They'd be fucking furious! What's with his name anyway? Pharrell? It sounds like a nasty skin rash! No chance ace, you can keep your modern music. I would rather shit in my own hands and clap than listen to that rubbish!"

With her father, uncle and 80s Dave making their way back to Barry's, her destination had been chosen for her. The only route she could take without being caught was to turn left towards Runcorn Hill.

A former sandstone quarry, Runcorn Hill was once sourced to produce stone used to build Liverpool Cathedral and New York Harbour. It was now a park and nature reserve, used mostly by dog walkers and nature lovers. It was also Emily's route to pursue Jonathon's killer.

Hastily she ran into the heavily wooded grounds; choosing to leave the designated pathway and move through the harsh terrain to shorten her journey. She clambered upwards, pushing through the twisted undergrowth and gnarled branches. In little time she found herself in an opening atop Runcorn Hill, looking down on to Weston

Road and her uncle's house. She hadn't meant to, Emily never wanted to see it again but her position had also given her a clear view of the lamppost where Jonathon had been brutally torn apart by zombies. Only he was gone and all that remained was the bodies of the two deaders that attacked him.

Looking down to the lamppost she allowed herself a glimmer of hope that Jonathon was somehow still alive and had managed to drag himself away from the road. Even though she knew deep down that was impossible, now that the thought had entered her head she had to check it out and so she began her descent, down through more of the thick, winter ravaged overgrowth, towards a dirt path where she was faced with three zombies, devouring the remains of a large man.

Smelling fresh meat the hungry zombies lifted their gaunt, blood soaked faces out of the man's enormous carcass and turned to face Emily who rather than wait for the rotters to come to her, was purposefully marching forward. She had somewhere she needed to be and she wasn't about to let three shufflers slow her down.

She swung the hammer into the forehead of the nearest shuffler killing it instantly. Blood, brain and cracked bone sprayed through the air as the zombie fell heavily to the floor with Emily's hammer wedged into the side of its head. Placing her foot on the zombie's chest she yanked the hammer free and swung the weapon again and then again, inflicting the same injuries to the others before running from the path and turning onto the road. There she found several other zombies sporadically shuffling towards her. As she approached, one by one they fell to her hammer. Nothing was going to get in her way.

She reached the lamppost where Jonathon was murdered and scanned the area. He was nowhere to be seen. In his place was a large pool of blood crystallised by the cold winter weather. Shiny droplets of plasma leading away from the lamppost presented a trail for her to follow. A trail which she soon realised was taking her to her uncle's house.

She nervously walked down the steep steps and stood outside the front door, looking upon her family home. She had no memory of her grandparents or the first years of her life when she lived there before her dad bought the house she grew up in. But she knew that it was a happy home, full of love and great memories. Now it was nothing but blackened bricks and mortar. A burnt out shell that barely resembled the beautiful house it once was.

She pushed open the front door and stepped inside. There, directly in front of her she found Jonathon, lying peacefully in the burnt out hallway. Scraped into the ash and dirt next to him were the words 'R.I.P. Skinny Jeans'.

Emily broke down and wept. Tears flowed freely as she lifted Jonathon's head to her chest and held him in a loving embrace. She stayed like that for some time, cradling him close, not wanting to let him go. Then she remembered her promise to make the man responsible pay and with a heavy heart she lay him back down, kissing him gently on his forehead.

Wiping tears from her eyes she opened the back door and entered the garden. There she saw the dismantled mountain of dead zombies and the dug up opened container. She smiled. Emily had known all about her uncle's zombie apocalypse stash. He had made sure she knew the exact location of every apocalypse stockpile in his garden.

"Now remember Emily love. If it's robots then dig by the back door, alien's over by the thorn bush, zombies in the middle, natural disasters such as earthquakes, floods and tornados the left of the shed, talking gorillas by the right of the shed, Reptile people that have lived underground for thousands of years over in the far left corner, killer clowns over there, giant man eating wasps over here and bloodsucking vampires right at the back."

"I love you Uncle Butty!" she smiled.

Picking up a shovel she clambered over the scattered zombies to reach the far end of the garden. There she began to dig. She only had to unearth the top layer of soil to know she was in the right place. The strong smell of garlic was a giveaway. Soon she had reached a large container with the words "Vampire Apocalypse' scrawled across the top.

Inside the container she found a top layer of large rotting garlic bulbs. Lifting her jacket to cover her mouth and nose, she removed the decaying bulbs as quickly as she could, revealing a layer of ready-made jarred minced garlic. Then below that there was garlic powder, garlic sausage and garlic bread and below those she found a large box containing over fifty bottles of holy water, complete with a letter of authenticity from the 'Israeli River Jordan Water Blessing Company'.

"You can buy anything online these days," she said to herself.

Finally, after removing the layers of rotting garlic products and almost certainly fake holy water Emily found what she was looking for.

Stakes.

Butty had made and stashed a large arsenal of small hand held wooden stakes, complete with an over the shoulder open topped bag, similar to an archer's quiver. Emily filled the quiver with as many stakes as possible and placed it over her shoulder. Then she heard the approaching rumble of motorbikes accompanied by cheering and yelling.

Through a small gap in the garden fence she peered through, looking to the street outside.

Four motorbikes approached. The bike leading dragged a man along the road, tied by rope, his clothes were torn and skin badly grazed due to friction from him skimming along the rough tarmac. Behind the motorbikes, a woman drove a large coach.

"Ok that should do it!" the man leading yelled, bringing his vehicle to a halt.

The leader dismounted his bike and removed his helmet to reveal a bald head covered in tattoos of flames. His companions followed his lead and parked their vehicles to surround the man tied to the rope.

"Please, I can't take any more. I'll do it, I'll do whatever you want me to just please don't drag me along anymore," the man cried.

The leader nodded towards the woman driving the coach. She was tall and dressed head to toe in biker's leathers, sporting a shaved head also covered in tattoos. She threw the coach keys to her leader.

"We want you to drive the coach, that's all. Nothing more and nothing less. Oh apart from that it will be on fire and full of zombies. Hahaha! Let's start herding the undead guys!" the man howled with laughter before removing a large bag from a canopy secured to the back of his motorbike.

"You remember your wife?" he snarled, unzipping the bag and spilling out the chopped up body parts of a woman.

The man tied to the rope vomited heavily and began wailing in despair. The bikers laughed hysterically.

"Billy, open up the back of the coach and the rest of you grab some body parts. This here is zombie chum and we're going to lure us some dead fuckers into the back of the coach. Hey Johno! You got the petrol canister?" the leader asked.

"Right here Paul!" came the reply.

"Come on then let's get a move on. Deano, start taking bets on how far the coach gets before it crashes. Winner gets beak or pills courtesy of our former employer wherever the bastard may be. Fucking dead with any luck!" the leader jeered.

Emily sat quietly with her back against the fence, listening to the groans of the undead and the laughter from the bikers as zombies were lured onto the coach. She knew that she needed to stay completely still so not to attract attention from the sadistic survivors or the zombies. It was harrowing and the wailing from the man made to watch his slaughtered wife be used as zombie bait chilled her.

After what felt like the longest time, the motorbikes began to rumble and the coach revved its engine. Finally they were gone and Emily could make her move.

"Three days into a zombie apocalypse and this town has turned into a Mad Max movie. Welcome to the friggin' Thunderdome!" she said, running from the garden.

Emily bounded up the steep stone steps at the front of the house. With hate in her heart she ran in the direction the blue transit van had taken the night previously. All the while thinking about what she was going to do to the man that murdered Jonathon and the ways in which she was going to inflict pain measurable to the grief she was feeling. And she was going to enjoy every minute of it.

All she had to do was find him.

Journal Entry 15

"Are we ever going to be able to move fifty yards without encountering zombies or lunatics? Check out this pair of hungry hippos!" Dave shouted from the Volvo Estate.

We had only been in Weston Point for two minutes and already we were at a standstill. Two cars had ploughed into each other blocking the road ahead. Both driver doors were open and the bodies of the owners lay shredded and torn in the road. Two obese zombies knelt over them, greedily sucking down their remains.

"Dave and I will take care of these two, you keep the engine running. They are big, clumsy and pre-occupied with the road kill they're eating. A swift blow from behind with this cricket bat and Dave's Battle Paddle should do it. Once they're down we should be able to push forward and nudge our way through those cars with ease. Even Dave's knackered old Volvo shouldn't have an issue," I told Butty who was smiling at me proudly.

"Fuck off!" I said, leaving the vehicle.

I knew why he was smiling. For years Butty had been grooming me and Emily for a zombie apocalypse. Just when it looked like I was a lost cause I surprise both him and myself by assessing a situation the same way he would and furthermore, the thought of killing the undead, for the first time, hadn't made me want to puke my guts up. But now I was filled with a different kind of dread. Dread that I might be slowly turning into my brother!

"Give me a hand Dave," I said approaching the Volvo.

"My pleasure kidda, just let me grab me paddle and I'll be with you quicker than a fart in a yoga class," he replied.

We approached the two grossly obese zombies. My god they were disgusting. It was like watching a pair of shaved grizzly bears bent over with their arses in the air.

"Which one do you want ace? The one with the builders arse big enough to park a bike or the one that inspired Sir Mix a-Lot to write Baby Got Back?" Dave so eloquently described.

I didn't reply but instead dashed forward and battered the head of the zombie with the builders arse into a bloodied mush. Dave was taken aback by my assertiveness and followed suit, drilling the Battle Paddle through the head of Baby Got Back.

When yanking the paddle from the zombie's head, the force Dave applied flopped the obese shuffler onto its back, revealing the deader's enormous stomach to have ruptured open. Man it was revolting. This zombie had literally eaten until it had burst. Then I heard a horrific gargling nose, like a bird choking to death. It was Dave's stomach rumbling. I looked at him in disbelief.

"What? I'm fucking starving lar. I've not eaten since last night and smokes, although delicious, are no substitute for a decent meal. Just looking at the size of this woman is making me think of all the food she must have eaten to get that big. I mean come on John, look at that exploded stomach and tell me it doesn't make you fancy a curry? Or even better, a massive blancmange or trifle. It looks a bit like a trifle actually. Sure the custard has curdled a bit but I'd still give it a go. Yep, a big delicious trifle all nicely presented inside a huge fleshy bowl. I could just dip me paddle in lar and have a taste!" he drooled.

"Dave you are a sick man, have I ever told you that?" I squirmed, scrunching my face in disgust.

"Definitely more than once Ace but it will take a lot more than a massive zombie with a busted open belly to put me off my grub. Come on let's get out of here before I actually convince myself her stomach is a pudding and I get stuck in. I've got a tin of your brother's spam in the car. If I concentrate hard enough whilst eating it I can maybe imagine it's a cheese burger or a mixed grill," he envisaged, rubbing his belly.

"You can imagine it's a five star Michelin meal prepared by Gordon Ramsey for all I care. I can't think about food till we've found Emily. Butty and I will push through these cars with the Land Rover. You tuck into your spam or whatever you imagine it to be then follow behind," I instructed, walking back to the vehicle.

"OK chief. Do you know you sounded just like your nutty brother then?" Dave smiled.

"Fuck Off!" was my reply.

Dave pulled the Volvo to the side and Butty drove the Land Rover forward, pushing through the two car barricade with ease.

The vehicles slowly parted to reveal a man standing defensively in the road, staring at us whilst nervously clutching a knife. He was surrounded by bodies and was wearing a Poundland uniform. Also in the road ahead, beyond the man in the road, were pockets of zombie activity. Small gatherings of the undead formed crowds at various points along the street. Something had their attention.

"Don't even think about getting out of the car John. We're just going to drive around him, don't even make eye contact. If he comes for us, then we take him out. The quicker we get away from him and those zombies up ahead the better." Butty said firmly.

Slowly we moved around the man with Dave following behind us. I did as Butty had asked and made no eye contact but I could feel him watching us, ready to defend himself if need be. Within seconds we had driven passed, ready to continue our search for Emily when the man suddenly called out.

"Wait!" he yelled.

We heard Dave bring the Volvo to a halt. Butty was not amused. Against his better judgement he stopped the vehicle then slammed his fists into the stirring wheel, shaking his head in disapproval.

"That retro chain smoking smart arse is going to be the death of us! This isn't a good idea John, we don't need anyone else tagging along. He's only going to slow us down and with zombies close by that's the last thing we need," he groaned.

"I think Dave has already decided we do need someone else and I think he's right. That could quite easily be one of us needing help," I replied opening the passenger door, "Shout if you see any zombies coming."

"We don't know the first thing about him, he could be a complete nut job?" Butty replied with concern.

Well if the situation wasn't so god damn depressing I would have pissed myself laughing. My brother, winner of Runcorn's Craziest resident award for twenty years running was concerned about nut jobs!

"Well then he'll fit right in won't he?" I quipped, slamming the car door.

Dave and I approached the man cautiously and for a short while we all stood in silence. His complexion was so pale he was practically white and he was shaking and jittered nervously. Whoever this guy was it was obvious he had been through a traumatic experience. It was difficult to know what to say to him and just when I thought we'd be stood in silence for eternity, Dave approached the man, lit two cigarettes and offered one to him which was gratefully accepted.

"So what the fuck happened here then?" Dave asked, as sensitive as always!

"They killed them, all of them," the man quivered.

"Zombies?" I asked.

"No, not zombies. People. We had been hiding out in the Shopping City, in Poundland where I work. Me, Tin Tin and Neil. But we decided to leave to come here, to Neil's house so he could be with his family. It was meant to be safe here but we should never have left, we should never have left Poundland!" he cried, quickly turning hysterical.

"Just calm down Ace, take a toke on the bifter and relax. What's your name kid?" Dave asked.

51

"Steven," he said, coughing his name following a long pull on the cigarette.

"My name's Dave but you can call me Cool Bastard for short and this is John. The guy looking agitated in the Land Rover over there is Butty but don't worry about him. He might be a few sandwiches short of a picnic but he's alright really. Tell us more about what happened Stevie lad," Dave said.

"The drive here was relatively easy. We had to manoeuvre our way around crashed and abandoned vehicles, dodge a few zombies but nothing got in our way. The roads were pretty quiet. Until we arrived here that is. We pulled into the street to find three men looting houses. If they came across any survivors they were dragging them from their homes and tying them to lamp posts, using them as bait for the undead. Zombies would eat those tied up and the looters could go about their business. Look behind you. That's what you can see further up the street," Steven said.

Dave and I turned our heads and gave the small gatherings of zombies a closer inspection. Steven was right! Behind us we saw zombies had crowded around the bodies of survivors tied to almost every lamp post and telegraph pole on the street, feasting on their remains. The bodies that didn't have zombies chewing on them had already been gobbled and were now barely recognisable as human. The look of dread on my face caught Butty's attention and he took a closer inspection also.

"When we arrived it was too late for Neil's family. His brother, sister in law, his son and his pregnant wife… they were all being eaten alive. We did everything we could to save them but it was too late. No sooner had we killed all the zombies the three men appeared and attacked us from behind, knocking us out and tying us up like everyone else. I came round as one of the men, a big guy covered in food stains, was tying my arms around the lamp post. He was crying, I could tell he was being forced to act against his will. He lent in close and placed a knife in my hands and whispered "I'm sorry." Then he moved away. I waited until the three men had gone then cut myself free, managing to escape just before zombies got me. Tin Tin and Neil were not so lucky."

"Can you describe the men that did this?" I asked.

"The one in charge was smaller than the others and had a rucksack on his back. He's the one that killed Neil and Tin Tin. The other two guys? The one that helped me was really big, I mean he was huge and like I said, with food stains all over his clothes. The other guy was average build and height, middle aged I think. It's all a bit of a blur. I took a nasty fall yesterday and my head has been hazy ever since. I think I have a concussion," Steven informed.

"Did they drive a blue van?" I asked.

"Yeah I think they did, a blue transit. Wait a minute you know these guys?" Steven said with worry, clutching his knife tightly before dizziness set in and he stumbled, falling to one knee.

"Hey relax, it's ok. We're not going to hurt you. We do know these people but it's not what you think. The one in charge, he burnt our house down yesterday and killed my daughter's boyfriend. She's missing, out looking for revenge. That's what we're doing now, we're trying to find her," I said.

"And that rucksack ace, it's got a head in it. A proper manky one too! Trust me, it's got more scabs than Russell Brand's dick," Dave added.

"Come with us, even if it's just till you get over your concussion. You won't last the day out here on your own. Safety in numbers." I smiled, placing a hand on Steven's shoulder.

"What are you going to do when you find your daughter? Are you going after the men with the van? If you do, then I want part of it. My whole life I've been scared. Scared to stand up to people, scared to grasp opportunity, scared to live. But not anymore. If there's one thing I've learnt these last few days it's to do what needs to be done and those guys need to pay for what they did. They're worse than the zombies and if they're to get what they deserve then I want in!" Steven replied, his anger and upset clear for us to see.

I placed my arm around him and we walked to our car. I could see Butty shaking his head in the driver's seat, obviously annoyed that our scouting party had grown in numbers but I couldn't have cared less. If we were to find Emily we needed all the help we could get. Plus Steven was alone and we had a common enemy. It made sense for us to stick together. Butty would come round, once he had finished sulking!

"Butty meet Steven. The man that killed Jonathon murdered his friends so he's coming with us, OK?" I said forcefully, taking a seat in the back of the Land Rover with our new companion.

Steven reached out for a hand shake but Butty didn't accept. Instead he growled and muttered something under his breath whilst glaring at me disapprovingly through the rear view mirror.

"Ignore Captain Insane. He only puts up with me because I'm his brother and he has no choice, otherwise he'd quite happily use me as zombie fodder," I said.

Dave honked the horn of his Volvo and motioned for us to get a move on, resulting in my brother flicking him the 'V' sign before starting the engine and pulling away.

The road ahead was littered with corpses, abandoned cars and the shuffling dead, many of which had finished guzzling down the remains of the poor bastards used as bait and were now showing interest in our vehicles. It was slow and difficult going and we were making very little progress in our mission to find Emily. Everything was slowing us down and zombies banging up against the car and slapping their rotting hands against the windows made it almost impossible for us to search. We could have passed Emily several times over and we wouldn't have noticed. Now the evening was drawing in and the chances of us finding her today were lessening. Soon we would need to find somewhere secure to hold up for the night. I had never felt so useless and Butty sensing my anguish decided to offer a few words of comfort.

"You feel helpless don't you? Don't worry little brother, I have every confidence that our Emily is just fine. I've trained her well and there's nothing in this hell of a world she can't handle. If it was you out there on your own then, well, that would be a completely different story. We would have no doubt presumed you dead hours ago and turned in for an early night," he said.

If it wasn't for the music coming from 80s Dave's car I probably would have cried. But it's difficult to feel upset with What's New Pussycat booming into your ears.

The Taking of the Pavilions

All through the night the battle had raged. The green grass of the sports fields were now a deep red from the blood of the fallen and undead alike.

The Pavilions had been set up as a safe house for survivors. Somewhere for the Weston Point residents of Runcorn to hole up and wait for help to arrive. With little to no knowledge of what they were dealing with, it had not taken long for their 'safe house' to become compromised and soon the walking dead had infiltrated their ranks and chaos ensued.

To their credit, The Pavilions had set up a screening area to check survivors for scratches, bite marks or any other visible sign of infection. Anyone found to be infected was denied entry, much to the distress of everyone involved and of course, the family members and friends that watched their loved ones be turned away. They were unprepared and overwhelmed by how many survivors needed shelter. All it took was for a mother to smuggle her young son with a small scratch to his knee through the screening process and within a few hours of opening its doors, the infection had breached their walls and the battle for survival began.

For almost two days survivors held off the dead but in the end it was the dead that won and the large sports club had become a living morgue with hundreds of zombies populating its grounds.

Only the crazy or fearless would dare attempt to take The Pavilions for the own.

"I've done a bad thing Ed, I've done a bad thing …"

Tom rocked himself backwards and forwards in the passenger seat of the blue transit van, arms wrapped around his stomach with tears rolling down his cheeks. He wore his heart on his sleeve and his distress at everything Ged had forced him to do was clear to see. Since the zombie outbreak he had witnessed and been an accessory to arson, burglary and murder. "Kill or be killed!" Ged would say followed by a threat that if he did not do as instructed, it would be him that would be burnt alive or tied up and fed to hungry zombies.

Ed placed an arm around his friend's huge shoulders. In part this was to offer support but mostly because he hoped the gesture would calm Tom enough to lower his voice. The last thing they needed right now was for their volatile boss to sense weakness within his team.

"We've both done bad things, Tom, but that doesn't make us bad people," he said softly, "We're just doing what we have to do to survive that's all."

"Why does he make us do it?" Tom blubbed.

"I don't know, Tom. It's a different world we live in now. Nice people like you that see the good in everyone and always want to do the right thing, they don't make it in this world. Crazy bastards like Ged, they're top of the food chain now. He's shown that he will do anything to survive. Kill or be killed he says. It's survival of the craziest and lucky for us we know the craziest bastard there is. The best thing for us right now is to fall in line and do exactly as he says but it won't be forever I promise you that. Here, eat this," Ed said, handing him a tin of corned beef, "Don't let Ged know I gave this to you, OK?"

Tom's upset lessened as his chubby hands fumbled with the tin of his favourite food. Eating always brought him comfort.

Outside of the van, on the other side of the road close to the entrance for the large grounds of The Pavilions stood Ged, smoking a cigarette with a bloodied sword in hand and a collection of slaughtered zombies at his feet. More were approaching. Over his shoulder he carried the rucksack containing his cousin's head.

He faced the oncoming shufflers and stood his ground as they staggered within grabbing distance. With the sword gripped tightly in both hands he watched as one by one the deaders sniffed the air around him then shuffled past ignoring his presence completely. Instead they headed towards Tom and Ed. A smirk spread across his face and he casually strolled towards his companions, slicing the heads from the necks of every zombie in his path.

"He's coming," Ed began hastily, "don't let him see the food I gave you. He'll only lose his temper and limit your supplies even more."

Tom turned to Ed and licked the last smearing of corned beef out of the tin, offering his friend a satisfied grin. Like a hungry dog he had guzzled and licked the tin completely clean, leaving no evidence of his tasty treat.

"Out of the van, both of you," Ged instructed.

With several zombies still approaching they reluctantly left the vehicle and scurried behind their boss, watching as he decapitated those that remained. Then one by one he dragged every rotting body into the road, creating a circle.

"The things you find in people's houses," he said, admiring the blood covered blade. "Come, stand inside the circle with me, don't worry about your weapons you won't need them. The house I burnt down last night got me thinking. Why was it covered in zombie limbs? Every exterior wall was covered with rotting arms, legs, hands and feet but why? To ward off intruders? In part maybe but they didn't keep me away. Then again, I am a special kind of crazy! No, the real reason for those fuckers decorating their house with zombie parts my stupid and spineless friends, was to mask the smell of the living. Come here and I'll show you."

Ed with Tom following, acted on their bosses instructions and entered the circle of the dead. Once inside they waited nervously for shufflers to arrive.

Slowly several zombies staggered from the grounds of The Pavilions and headed their way. Tom closed his eyes and made fists with both of his enormous hands, squeezing tightly in an attempt to stop himself from crying. Ed remained strong, standing tall with his chest puffed out so not to show how scared he was to his boss. Ged leant on his sword. His crazy eyes big and wide with excitement as every zombie shuffled around the circle, stopping occasionally to sniff the air only to then walk away. It was as if the three men did not exist and Ed's fear was soon replaced with astonishment. Astonishment because his boss was right!

"Incredible!" Ed gasped.

"Now what to do with this discovery? What was that Joni?" Ged said looking over his shoulder to his rucksack, "The Pavilions? What a fantastic idea!"

The three of them stepped out of the circle of bodies and walked to the entrance of The Pavilions, gazing upon the zombie infested fields. Ged moved forward and slayed a small group of nearby deaders before turning to his companions.

"Beautiful isn't it?" he grinned, "All we have to do is kill every single one of them and The Pavilions will be ours. The smell from the hundreds of rotting corpses will keep us protected, from both the living and the dead. That will be both our home and centre for operations. We're in the looting business now boys. Runcorn is dead and ours for the taking and take it we will. Starting with Weston Point we'll loot every house in the area until there's nothing worth taking left. If we come across any other survivors then, well... we know what we need to do don't we? Exactly what we did to the boy last night and the people earlier. It's kill or be killed now boys. The old world wasn't ready for Ged Woods but my God, I'm built for this one! Mark my words this town is going to be ours, starting with The Pavilions!"

"There's too many boss, it's impossible. How are we going to kill so many zombies without them attacking us?" Ed asked, overwhelmed by the task at hand.

Ged moved forward once again, approaching the small group of deaders he had previously dispatched. Using his sword he sliced open the stomach of one of the zombies and knelt down beside it, reaching inside the open wound to remove intestines. Then he smeared them across his body, covering his torso in congealed blood.

"We will do what needs to be done," he said rubbing his blood dripping hand across his face, "Catch," he added, throwing Ed and Tom a sliced up zombie part each, "Smear yourself with as much blood as you can. If you need any more just ask, we have plenty of supplies!"

Tom's bottom lip began to quiver and he looked to Ed with an expression that pleaded for him not to go through with it. No words were exchanged, only an apologetic look from Ed as he smeared zombie gloop across his friend's overcoat before applying it to himself.

Over his shoulder Ed heard muttering and turned to see Ged with Joni's head in his hands, he was discussing battle plans with his deceased cousin.

"I look and smell like the bad men Ed, I don't like this," Tom whined.

"I don't like it either my friend but it's better smelling and looking like them then actually being one. Here, have a chocolate bar that will cheer you up," Ed replied offering the big guy a Snickers.

"No I'm not hungry. This smell is putting me off my food and that has never happened before, EVER. Even when granddad Jim needed his nappy changing I could still eat. Or when my old dog Henry farted I could still eat and those used to make Auntie Maureen cry! What if I lose my appetite all together and I don't like corned beef anymore. What will I do Ed? I don't think I can live without corned beef!" Tom threatened.

"Ed, Tom! Joni has a plan. Bring the van into The Pavilion's grounds. We're going to test its suspension!" Ged proclaimed a grin as large as his ego and a glint in his eye as bright as his heart was black.

As always, Ed and Tom did as they were told and brought the van through the entrance of The Pavilions' grounds. Ged opened the driver's door and clambered inside, pushing Ed into the passenger seat next to Tom. He removed Joni's head from the rucksack and placed him on the dashboard, looking out of the windscreen.

Ged howled a maniacal laugh and revved the engine.

"Hold on tight boys, this could get bumpy!" he yelled.

The van sped forward rumbling into the sports fields, ploughing into zombie after zombie. The noise from the undead hitting the body of the vehicle was deafening. Loud bangs made it sound like the van had come under heavy gun fire and Tom shielded his ears with his hands; his large body rocking from side to side, crashing into Ed as the van tumbled over the many bodies. Ged was loving every minute of the mayhem. Laughing and cheering with every zombie he mowed down.

Eventually the damage sustained to the van brought it to a halt. Now it was time to get hands on and following Ged's lead, Tom and Ed, albeit battered and bruised from the rough ride, left the vehicle and assessed the damage. By this point the majority of the zombies had been run down and the fields were a sea of twisted and twitching bloodied bodies. Ged marched forward, stabbing his sword into the heads of the undead as they lay in the grass. The remaining zombies that had avoided a collision with the van were alert and excitable from the disturbance, moaning and roaming around the grounds manically but without direction.

Smearing themselves in the blood of the dead was working and the three men commenced their hands on attack, destroying the heads of every zombie still standing and finishing off those squirming on the ground.

For Ed and Tom it was a long and difficult day. Ged on the other hand was revelling in his murder spree and looked to have the energy to do it all again if need be. But by late afternoon the fields were clear and not affording his men any rest, Ged stormed towards the large Social Club, ready to clear its interior.

"We're beat boss, we need to rest for a while. We can't do anymore," Ed rasped, his breath heavy from exertion.

Filled with anger Ged turned to his men, marching towards them with his sword pointing forwards, ready to threaten them into doing his bidding. Then a distant rumbling noise caught his attention, increasing in volume with every second. All three men looked to the entrance of The Pavilions' grounds as four motorbikes appeared, stalling momentarily before riding into the fields and pulling up in front of them.

The lead biker removed his helmet revealing his flame tattooed head. He assessed the hundreds of dead zombies then looked the three men up and down.

"Hello Ged. Where's Joni?" the lead biker asked.

"He's over there in the van," Ged replied, nodding towards the vehicle.

The bikers looked at the van to find Joni's rotting scabby head on the dashboard glaring back at them.

"We assumed you were dead?" the biker smirked, turning back to Ged.

"Ah Paul Hillan, you always underestimate me! I see you've got Billy, Kitty, Johno and Deano with you. I wondered what had happened to the rest of my staff. Being close to useless I had thought you were dead too but good job, you proved me wrong. Now come on we've got work to do. Help me clear the inside of The Pavilions," Ged instructed, turning to walk to the building.

"We don't work for you anymore. We're our own men now. Thanks for clearing the fields and doing all the hard work but we'll take it from here and if you don't like that then, well..." the lead biker replied.

The bikers brandished an array of knives and bats and displayed them proudly. Both Ed and Tom backed away, keen to show they did not want any trouble.

"Hold on, hold on. There's no need for any of that," Ged said approaching Paul, "We've known each other a long time. For years you have all served me well. You have sold my drugs and done my bidding without discourse. So now you want go out on your own? I can understand that. It's a new world full of wonder and excitement. The only problem is it's not your world. It's mine!"

Ged swung his sword quickly, removing Paul's head from his body in one clean slice.

Stunned, the other bikers sat like statues on their vehicles with their mouths open wide. Their eyes followed Paul's head as it bounced and rolled along the bloodied grass before resting at Ged's feet. He bent down and with his free hand pushed two fingers into Paul's eye sockets and a thumb in his mouth, carrying the decapitated head like a bowling ball.

"So, who would like to be next? Any volunteers?" he smiled, raising his sword in the air and swinging Paul's head with his other hand.

They all climbed off their vehicles and took a few steps towards Ged threateningly. Then they turned to each and one by one lowered their weapons.

"Whatever you want boss, we're with you." Billy said, submissively.

Ged smiled an evil teeth baring grin and led them inside the Pavilions. Ed smiled also. Not because he was pleased to have his colleagues back in the fold. He knew them for what they were. The lowest of the low. Cowardly opportunists that needed direction and easily ruled by fear.

With these guys back in the group, Ged would pay less attention to both himself and Tom. There was now a real chance that they could escape his evil employer's grasp.

The mangled body of a zombie began to twitch, lifting its head out of the grass and into the air. Like it was a ten pin bowling ball Ged swung Paul's head, sending it rolling with speed along the field before hitting the twitching zombie in the face, knocking it back into the grass.

"Strike!" Ged cheered.

Journal Entry 16

"Everybody hates their job. It's not unusual for somebody to dislike what they do for a living you know!" I snapped.

It was dusk and the search for Emily had temporarily been put on hold so we could find somewhere secure to hole up for the night. I wasn't happy about it but Butty had reassured me it was the right thing to do and that Emily, if she had remembered her apocalypse training, would be doing the same. Adding to my misery was 80s Dave who, since we had left our vehicles to inspect a few houses, had taken it upon himself to question my mayonnaise tasting career.

"Yes Ace, but your job was tasting my mayonnaise and making a decision if it was good enough to go on the shelves for people to buy. I've watched you eat mayo kid. You have a face like a Bulldog chewing on a nettle. You'd have a better time getting your rectum examined by the Incredible Hulk! How the fuck you can run a quality check on mayonnaise when you can't stand the stuff is beyond me," he questioned.

"Easy. If it looks like congealed walrus jizz, smells like eggy farts and tastes like tippex then it's fine. Oh and please don't refer to my job as tasting your mayo. The only good thing about the apocalypse is I don't have to work at the bloody mayonnaise factory anymore. Don't ruin it by making me imagine I had been tasting your junk," I gagged.

"Well firstly, how you know what congealed walrus jizz looks like I don't know and nor do I want to but I can assure you that my jizz looks nothing like that. It looks more like wall paper paste, smells like digestive biscuits and tastes like, well... fuck knows. Benson & Hedges probably. And secondly, you can dress it up however you want Ace but at the end of the day I made mayonnaise and you had to eat it. I produced and you consumed," Dave stated.

"I think I'm gonna be sick," Steven interrupted, heaving into a nearby bush.

Butty had moved ahead of us to scout potential places for us to stay and I could see him shaking his head and mumbling something about having two weak bellied throw up merchants and an extra from Footloose to look after.

"Sorry about that," Steven apologised, "I'm still concussed and all that talk of your biscuit sperm sent me over the edge. Zombies I'm just about getting used to but hearing about your sperm I can do without," he added, wiping puke from his chin.

"Sorry Stevie lad. Put your fingers in your ears as I can't guarantee such references won't crop up again. But anyway, as you know John, unlike you, I liked working in the mayo factory. The hours were good, money was alright, the work was a piece of piss and I got to talk bollocks all day. What more could I have asked for?" Dave grinned, remembering his job fondly.

"Well the talking bollocks bit is true. You could give my brother a run for his money with the crap you harp on about. What was it you were blabbering about the other day? When werewolves turn back into their human form where does all the hair go? And if people really want to know if the Loch Ness Monster is real, they should just test the water for monster piss," I replied.

"That's not bollocks Ace, those are questions that really need answering. I bet Stephen Hawkins can't find the answer to the werewolf one and testing Loch Ness for monster piss is just common sense. Drives me up the wall when you see these so called monster hunters with millions of pounds worth of equipment and they never find anything. Just test the river for piss! I guarantee they'll find their answer!" he informed, like a man that had discovered the meaning of life.

"Oi! Statler and Waldorf, keep the noise down will you and hurry up. I think I've found somewhere," Butty interjected, inspecting the door of a large semi-detached house.

The house was positioned at the top of a small cul-de-sac and from the exterior the property looked immaculate, like the zombie apocalypse had ignored its existence. To the front of the house there was a gated driveway and to the side a large wooden gate giving access to a fenced rear garden.

"It's not over-looked and it's right at the top of the cul-de-sac looking down to the mouth of the road which puts us in the best defensive position should we come under attack. Now we need to break in without causing much damage to the door. Any ideas Dave?" Butty said.

"Hey lar, just because I'm a Scouser doesn't mean I know how to break into houses you know!" An insulted Dave yelled aggressively.

There was a silence following Dave's outburst as Steven and I kept quiet and Butty weighed up if Dave was really as annoyed as he appeared. Then the retro bum nugget let out a bellowing laugh.

"Ha ha ha! Only joking Ace! Of course I know how to break into a house. I was raised in Toxteth kid!" he chortled.

Dave swaggered towards the door whilst humming the theme tune from Hill Street Blues. He examined the door closely then crouched down, lifting the flap on the letter box.

"The first thing to do is check in the hallway. You'll be surprised how many morons leave their house keys near their front door. Now let's have a…."

As Dave peered through the letter box a broom handle poked through and jabbed him in the forehead, sending him backwards onto his arse.

"Don't even think about it. I'm like, 8ft tall and stuff. I'm dead hard and I've got guns so go away before you get hurt!" said the young male voice from inside the house.

"I'll handle this," Butty said confidently, "We are not looking for trouble but if you don't open the door right now, we will be forced to break it down and KILL YOU!"

"Great that Butty lad. Did you never fancy a job with the Samaritans or maybe as a police negotiator? You know, the ones they send into delicate situations to keep the peace?" Dave said rubbing his forehead.

Just as I was about to intervene and explain to the voice behind the door that we won't be killing anyone, the door opened quickly to reveal a petrified young man with his hands in the air and his legs trembling with fright.

"Please don't kill me!" the lad blubbed.

69

He must have been no more than eighteen years of age and he looked petrified but who wouldn't be? Three men just tried to break into his house and threatened to kill him. I'd be a little on the nervous side too!

"Put the mop down soft lad we're not going to hurt you. Well, Dave might if you stab him in the head with it again. We just need your living room for the night then we'll be gone," Butty said.

Butty was now in smug mode with a grin as wide as a Cheshire cat. Pleased that his threatening approach had been a success he puffed out his chest and barged past the quivering young man entering his home.

"Sorry about this mate and please, I know this is must be frightening but try to relax. Forget what my brother said, nobody is going to kill you. Butty has his own ways of doing things," I said, attempting to ease the man's concerns.

"Yeah, he went to the Charlie Manson Finishing School for Psychos! I'm Dave by the way, the fella you poked in the head with your broom handle. Luckily for you I'm hard as nails and it didn't hurt a bit but two inches lower and you would have bust my sunglasses, kid. Then I would have had to have killed you and unlike his brother I mean what I say!" Dave growled, following Butty into the house.

"My name is Steven, I work in Poundland and I watched the only person I have ever loved turn into a zombie and she didn't even know I existed. I also have a concussion and I threw up in your bushes because they were talking about walrus jizz. I don't know these people," Steven said, walking past the man into his house.

"And my name is John. Thanks for opening your door, even if it was only because you thought you were going to die. Like my brother said, we just need your living room. We've got our own food and water, we don't need anything else from you but somewhere safe to rest. We'll be gone first thing in the morning I promise," I assured the kid.

"You've been outside. What's it like out there? I haven't stepped out of the house," he said, regaining control of his nerves.

"I won't lie, it's fucking horrible. Corpses, both dead and undead are everywhere. Runcorn looks like a war zone and from what we know, it's like this every place else. You don't need to hear any of this, let's get this door closed and I can introduce you to everyone properly. You'll see we're not so bad really. What's your name kid?" I asked.

"Brittain, as in Great Britain but spelt B.R.I.T.T.A.I.N. My mother was an agoraphobic traveller too scared to leave the house. She wanted to see every inch of our land but never got further than the front door. That's why she called me Brittain. Unfortunately I too am agoraphobic. That's why I was asking you what it's like outside" he jittered, a nervous twitch making his eye pulse occasionally.

There are no normal people left in this world, they have all been eaten by zombies!

Inside The Wolfs Lair

"Hold my hand and don't let go unless I say so. Remember to keep your eyes on the floor at all times, can you do that for me? There are lots of very unpleasant things out here that you do not want to see," Nick said to Sophie firmly.

Sophie took Nick's hand and with baby Gaby resting snuggly against his chest in a baby sling fashioned from one of his Grandmother's scarfs, they exited Churchill Mansions, moving vigilantly towards Runcorn town centre. In her free hand Sophie held Teddy, swinging him backwards and forwards as she moved, fixing her eyes on the ground as instructed. She felt safe with Nick and he, for the first time in his life, felt like he had a purpose.

For as long as Nick could remember he had always been an outsider, never really conforming to the rules thrust upon him by society. His whacky clothes and outrageous hairstyles along with his impulsive and sometimes volatile personality, meant he found it difficult to settle in any one place and keeping friends had always been a problem. The one person that always saw the good in him was his Grandmother. He missed her love and kindness. Her warm smile, gentle words and caring nature always made him feel secure and more importantly, wanted. He had missed her greatly since the zombie outbreak but now in the touch of Sophie's hand and the warmth in her eyes, he once again felt the affection missing since his Grandmother's death.

"Where are we going, Uncle Nick? Can I call you Uncle?" Sophie asked.

"An old friend once told me about a man that knows everything there is about zombies and that if ever I find myself in danger, to go and see him so that's where we're heading and yes, of course you can call me Uncle Nick. You and little Gaby are my family now and I'm never going to leave you, no matter what," he smiled, kissing Gaby on her forehead.

Nick took the girls through the town centre with haste, heading on foot towards Weston Road, all the while keeping a look out for incoming zombies and for a possible vehicle they could use. The undead were plentiful but their meandering and slow shuffling was rarely a threat for Nick and Sophie's quick feet. Any that did encroach were welcomed with a swift stab to the head from the large knife he had brought with him as a weapon.

The further away from the Old Town and the closer to their destination they became, the more the scene changed. Shuffling zombies were replaced by slaughtered zombies, carpeting the roads and pavements with their corpses. Sophie could no longer keep her eyes fixed on the ground to avoid the hell that surrounded her.

"Close your eyes little one. Don't open them till I say so," Nick instructed, lifting her up and taking her in his arms.

She flung her arms around his neck and placed her head on his shoulder but she found it impossible to keep her eyes shut. Sophie had to see the extent of which Nick was trying to protect her from and she sneaked a look at the sea of dead people behind her. Sophie had hidden the memory of her father's tragic death at the beaks of the rabid zombie ducks and geese, in a distant corner of her mind. But this had brought those memories flooding back. She buried her head into Nick's chest and started to sob quietly.

With carefully placed steps Nick continued, striding and stretching over decaying zombies till finally their numbers decreased and he reached Weston Road. Ahead of him he saw a parked car, an old 1980s red Thunderbird and from his position it appeared in good condition.

He looked to the darkening sky. It was early evening and would soon be dark. With the undead corpses now behind him he let go of Sophie, placing her back onto her feet then from inside the make shift baby sling, Gaby began to cry.

"She needs her feed," Sophie said, reaching up to stroke her little sister's head.

"Just a little further. Then we'll be somewhere safe and your sister can have her bottle," he replied.

"Uncle Nick, I saw all those dead people. There was hundreds of them and we haven't seen real people since that horrible old lady and her son. What if we're the last people alive?" Sophie asked.

Nick smiled and knelt down, taking her by both hands.

"Oh there are others, I guarantee it and they'll be a lot nicer than that horrible old woman and her son too. When we find them I bet they'll have hot food, clean clothes and somewhere safe for us to stay. I bet there's even other kids for you to play with. Come on, let's get a move on before it gets dark. The house I'm looking for isn't far now. It's just past that old car parked ahead," he said.

They rushed towards the Thunderbird and Nick inspected it. On the floor of the driver's seat he saw several cigarette butts and a cassette tape labelled 'Dave's ultimate 80s synthtastic megamix Vol

17'. He was inspecting the vehicle's four flat tyres when Sophie called him over.

"Uncle Nick?" she called with concern.

Nick looked over to Sophie, who was stood at the top of steep steps leading down to a large house. The house and the large overgrowth that surrounded it had been burnt out. His heart sank and he hoped that he had got it wrong and this wasn't Lone Wolf's house. Then he noticed the charred remains of body parts nailed into the blackened bricks of the property and he knew he had found the right place.

Walking down the steps they approached the front of the house and looked upon the burnt and blackened heads of five zombies nailed to spike's outside the entrance. They barely resembled heads at all and looked more like overcooked chicken on kebab skewers. Nick removed Gaby from her sling and gave her to Sophie.

"Take your sister and wait here for a second, I need to look inside to see if there is anything we can take. The building might not be stable," he said.

"Is this the house where we were going to be safe?" Sophie asked.

"I'm afraid it is. Wait here, I won't be long I promise," Nick smiled, ruffling her hair with his hand.

He walked through the broken doorway and entered the house. The first thing that stood out, amidst the blackened interior and fire damaged walls, was that the stairway to the first floor had been removed. Recalling Believe Nothing's detailed descriptions of Lone Wolf, he was now in no doubt he had found the correct house.

"Clever bastard," he said to himself.

Cautiously he walked further into the house, to the back of the property where he came across a blanket covered body. Next to the body, written in soot where the words "R.I.P Skinny Jeans".

"I can smell pork. Salty pork!" Sophie proclaimed, startling Nick with her presence.

"I thought I told you to wait outside?" he asked, leading her away from the body.

"Gaby needs her feed, she can't wait any longer, she's getting grumpy," she informed.

Nick removed the rucksack from his back and pulled out a bottle of water, a baby bottle and some powdered milk before making up the formula and passing it to Sophie. Sophie's frown and judgemental eye did not go unnoticed.

"You have no idea what you're doing do you?" Sophie sighed, feeding her sister.

To Sophie's surprise, Gaby took the bottle and drank from it greedily leading Nick to offer a smug look as a response to his young companion's mocking.

"We shouldn't stay for long, this place doesn't look safe. The car outside is unlocked. The tyres are punctured which will make it difficult to drive but we can lock the doors. If I can start the engine then maybe the heater still works. That will keep us warm till morning. When Gaby has finished her bottle that's what we'll do. Tomorrow, we'll find a new place, with no zombies!" he smiled.

Journal Entry 17

It had been several hours since Brittain fearfully opened up his home, allowing us to take over his living room as a result of my brother's threat to kill him if he didn't. I think I've mentioned before how people skills are not Butty's greatest asset. Well scrap that because in this new world it would appear that his abrupt, no nonsense, tactless approach works a treat!

We had made ourselves at home in the living room which, with its large bay window, gave us a perfect view of the cul-de-sac and any danger that may come our way. In the several hours we had been here not once had our reluctant host come in to the room to talk to us, choosing instead to stand at the open doorway, biting his nails, twitching his eye and scratching his head nervously whilst watching Steven sleep, Dave smoke and Butty keep look out at the window. It was obvious our presence was causing him stress and attempting to put his mind at rest, I had tried several times to talk him into joining us so he could learn more about the motley crew that had invaded his home. Hopefully so he could see that we were actually good guys. But he would not acknowledge my requests with a response. Choosing instead to stare at us whilst twitching nervously. I was about to give it one more shot when out of the blue and startling us all, he rushed into the living room and quickly sat on the carpet next to me.

"OK, so I know who you are now. I've been watching you all for a while and I think I've got you all figured out. The man asleep, Steven, he is new to your group and has obviously been through an ordeal. I can tell by your body language that none of you know him very well and his quiet demeanour and shell shocked expression are

77

enough to show me that something bad has happened. I mean look at him, even though he's asleep he looks like he's about to cry," Brittain said quickly, with a twitch of his eye and the nervous scratching of his head.

Steven was well away, lost to a deep sleep he did not hear Brittian's words. Instead he tossed and turned on the couch, mumbling something about a girl called Jess and multi packs of Mini Cheddars for £1!

"You in the window with the crazy look in your eyes and the copy of Busty Lovelies wrapped around your forearms; Butty is it? I know you didn't really want to kill me but you would have done if you needed to. You're the kind of person that does what needs to be done to survive and to protect your group. Emotion and morals don't come into it," he continued, pointing at my brother.

Butty kept his eyes on the window during his character appraisal, smugly nodding his head in agreement. That was two out of two so far for Brittain and considering his nervous and erratic appearance, I was pleasantly surprised by his near perfect descriptions.

"You with the sunglasses and headphones on, listening to that weird tinny music. Did you say your name is Dave? You chain smoke and act the way you do because you think it gives you identity. You think that if you didn't act that way then people would know the real you and you're scared that when they see how lonely you are, they won't like you anymore and you'll lose the small number of friends you have," Brittain surmised.

Well Dave's face was a picture. His jaw fell open so wide he nearly dropped his ciggie. I have only seen that expression on his face once before and that was when he asked someone to name the greatest Scottish band of the 80s and out of all the possible answers such as Simple Minds, Big Country and Deacon Blue, they said Wet Wet Wet!

"Alright smart arse pipe down. If I wanted to be psychoanalysed I would have got married! And this music isn't weird. It's 'The Lexicon of Love' by ABC, one of the finest albums ever made. You kids today wouldn't know a good song even if Martin Fry rocked up in his gold suit and sang it to you! It's all One Direction these days and that bloody Kanya West or whatever her name is. Over produced drivel from fame hungry no marks. You want to treat your ears to a Walkman and a mix tape of some of the finest music from the greatest decade of all time, kid. The fucking 80s!" Dave snapped.

"And you, John," Brittain said, looking at me, "You're the glue that holds your group together. Without you, none of you would be here. Why else would they all be following you on a suicide mission to find your daughter? "

I can't say I was completely happy with him calling the search for Emily a suicide mission but he'd done a pretty good job sussing us out by all accounts. Not that Dave would agree and Butty seemed to have enjoyed his character assessment greatly judging by the proud expression on his face. I've never known anyone to take delight in being basically called an emotionless loon before but that's my brother for you!

"Well I need a drink after listening to that load of old shite. Lonely my arse! Got any booze in this house Europe, or whatever your name's supposed to be?" Dave sulked, exiting the living room in a nark.

With Dave gone, Steven snoring and Butty's attention taken with the window; Brittain, with more confidence in our company, began to press me for information about the world beyond his front door. It's hard to believe this kid had spent most of his life inside his house; his only connection to the outside world being the internet, and television. When your only source of information is the bilge and scare mongering forced upon us by mainstream media then it's no wonder his illness never improved. At first I held concerns that telling him everything that had happened to us would send his agoraphobia into overdrive and he would lock himself away in a cupboard for the rest of his life but then I thought, ah fuck it, what harm could it do? So I told him about Dave and I watching our boss become a zombie after shitting himself to death. Then how his head separated into two halves and I got my feet lodged in them like a pair of slippers. Then how we drove into my daughter's zombified friend and the impact separated her head from her shoulders and we watched it roll down the road. How we, ahem, 'saved' my daughter from the hordes of the undead at the Grange Comprehensive School and made it to my brother's place to find he had nailed zombie body parts to the house and stored a mountain of undead corpses in his back garden. Then how Butty and Dave risked life and limb to go shopping for cigarettes; Dave with a giant mayonnaise stirring paddle for protection and Butty with a lampshade around his neck and shin pads on his forearms. I then told him about the house fire and the bastard that killed Jonathon and how we were now looking for my daughter after she ran away to get revenge.

So much had happened in the last few days that the most hideous of situations are starting to feel normal and details were rolling of my tongue matter-of-factly. It took me a while to notice the poor kid had turned green and it was describing the mountain of decomposing zombies in my brother's back garden that proved to be the final straw. Brittain gagged and heaved heavily then a noise left his throat not too dissimilar to water bubbling through a blocked drain! He ran out of the living room holding his mouth in an attempt to keep the vomit in. By the horrendous sounds, he had just about made it to the kitchen sink before his hurling commenced!

"Good work little brother. I think it's safe to say that the kid won't be stepping outside anytime soon. Five minutes talking to you and his phobia and anxiety is the worst it's ever been. It wouldn't surprise me if he zips himself up into a suitcase and stores himself away for eternity," Butty remarked.

"Where do you think Emily is?" I asked with concern, ignoring his smart arse remarks.

"Oh she's close I can guarantee it and like us, she'll have no doubt found a place secure for the night. She's a clever girl is our Emily and even with revenge on her mind she'll know it's too dangerous to be out at night. With the power out visibility is poor and let's not forget how cold it is. If a zombie doesn't get you then the weather will. Try not to worry John, I know it's hard but she's a survivor just like the rest of us Diants. Always has and always will be," he replied.

The morning could not come quick enough.

F-T-B P2

"I reckon we can make it as a three piece, no problem. We'll have to start rehearsing straight away though, to make sure we're tight for our next gig. We don't want to let our fans down," Chris considered.

Ben and Ricky looked at him perplexed. Had they heard him correctly? It was difficult to hear anything over the hellish sounds of the many zombies, groaning and pounding against the small, dome shaped portable toilet they found themselves trapped inside.

"Next gig? Are you out of your tiny mind? We've been stuck inside this stinking shitter since yesterday, the door keeps opening by itself and we're surrounded by zombies. I don't think we'll be gigging anytime soon and as for owing it to our fans? Our fans are more interested in eating us than listening to our music! I don't think the undead are into rock music but should we ever make it out of this poo shed alive then maybe we can give them a free gig and find out!" Ben yelled frustrated.

It had been a long and arduous night for the boys from Faster than Bulls. Following the death of their friend and band mate Tim in the explosion that destroyed Rockwell's diner, they had taken to the streets in the hope of finding a way to escape this town from hell. But surrounded by zombies and in a town they knew very little about, they hadn't made it very far, taking shelter in the first place they found. A new, solar powered, energy efficient portable toilet close to Runcorn bus station. The dome-shaped toilet was the only thing left in the town with power much to the band's despair because to keep the door locked it needed 20p inserted into it every fifteen minutes. Ricky had decided to tackle this problem head on from the start by kicking the door lock repeatedly until it eventually broke. This hadn't secured the door but rather sent its mechanics haywire and instead of the door requiring money to stay closed every fifteen minutes it was now completely random and could open at any time!

The lock to the toilet door flashed green and an alarm sounded; an ear piercing 'BEEEEEEP' accompanied the door unlocking. As it slowly opened, the groans from the undead outside increased in volume.

"Fucking eco friendly portaloo. Trust us to take shelter in the only place left in Runcorn with power. I mean, a solar panelled shitter of all things!" Rick exclaimed.

Ben delved into his pocket and retrieved a small amount of change, placing 20p in the lock. "We've only got one coin left and that door could open at any time. We're going to have to come up with a plan unless you want to be lunch to the horde outside?"

"If only we had our instruments we could rehearse in here. It's a bit cramped but the acoustics are superb," Chris piped up, ignoring Ben completely.

Ben and Ricky hung their heads in despair.

Hours passed and thankfully the temperamental door had stayed closed because Ben, Ricky and Chris were no closer to devising a plan of escape. There was only one exit and running into the grabbing hands and hungry mouths of the many zombies outside and fighting their way out was not a workable option.

Ricky sat on the toilet, still wearing his polka dot dress from the day before. He flicked the tap over the sink on and off, stopping and starting the flow of water.

"I'd give anything for some food right now. Even sat here in this stinking toilet with its piss stained floor I could quite happily demolish a kebab, full English breakfast or a take away pizza, anything fatty and full of grease," he drooled.

"It would have to be something fancy for me," Chris joined in, "Something expensive and extravagant by a Michelin Starred chef like Heston Blumenthal."

"There's not a chance in hell I'd eat any weird concoctions put together by that complete weapon! The bloke is off his tits!" Ricky replied, "Bacon dessert? Egg ice cream? Fish eyeball cocktails? Not on my watch. I have a theory of how he makes these god awful creations. Have you heard of a film called The Human Centipede? It's about a weirdo that makes a daisy chain of people, joined together surgically mouth to arse. Well I reckon that's what goes on in Heston's kitchen. He's got his own Human Centipede which he force feeds any old muck and serves up what's crapped out at the end!"

Ricky's rant was met with a look of disgust from Ben whilst Chris was in deep thought, contemplating what he had heard.

"He'd have to have two Human Centipedes though, because of nut allergies," Chris said, to which Ricky nodded in agreement.

"I am trapped in a toilet with morons. Can we please concentrate on coming up with a plan of escape before we all die? I don't want my last conversation to be about shitting into people's mouths!"

BEEP!

The door unlocked and again started opening. Ben fumbled with the remaining 20p, dropping it to the floor. The coin rolled through Ricky's legs then rested behind the toilet. Ricky dove to the floor to find it, his dress rucking up over his waist and exposing his bottom. Chris and Ben pushed against the door as hard as they could in an attempt to stop it from opening.

"Bloody hell Ricky, why the hell aren't you wearing any underpants? Your arse looks like a bear that's been shot in the face!" Chris strained, "Get that coin will you!"

The groans from the undead increased in volume as the door slowly opened and sunlight beamed through the gap in the door, shining a beam of light on Ricky's exposed anus.

Zombie hands started to claw their way through the gap. Chris removed one of his winkle pickers and began smashing it into rotting hands; shredding skin and breaking fingers of each one as they reached inside the door.

"Got it!" Ricky proclaimed, rushing to the door then placing the 20p in the lock.

The door closed once more, and the noise of zombies muffled.

"No coins left. The next time that door opens, we're dead." Ben gulped.

The minutes felt like hours and the hours felt like days as Faster than Bulls stood facing the toilet door. Chris had now removed both of his winkle pickers and placed them over his hands with the pointed toe end displayed as a stabbing device. Ben had removed the taps from the sink and was brandishing them between his fingers like knuckledusters. Ricky had a toilet seat lid as a shield in one hand and a toilet brush in the other.

Preparing for battle they faced the door, staring at the lock, knowing that it could open at any moment and the fight for their lives would begin.

Then it happened, the light on the lock turned green.

BEEP!

The door opened and reaching hands became stretching arms. Then the bodies of the undead filled the doorway.

Chris was the first to react, stabbing his pointy shoes into the heads of as many zombies as he could; darkened sticky blood spurted from the newly created holes in their foreheads like brown sauce from a squeezy bottle.

Backing him up was Ben, throwing punch after punch to any zombie that escaped Chris's first line of defence. The sharp edged nose of the taps clenched in his fists broke through the rotting flesh of his attackers with relative ease and after several fast repetitive shots, the skulls soon cracked.

Behind Ben, stood on the toilet was Ricky, thwarting shufflers that came close with his make shift shield and stabbing the toilet brush at anything he could.

Their defence, surprisingly, was working and very soon the doorway became blocked, jammed from bottom to top with dead zombies.

Nothing could get through but the dead, they kept on coming, pushing forward in their droves and the small portaloo started to shake.

"There's too many of them, they're going to topple it over!" Ricky yelled.

"Hit the floor!" Ben instructed.

The three of them crouched down low and huddled together on the floor, pushing themselves against the dead rotters in the doorway. The pressure from the horde ploughing forward, caused the portaloo to wobble, creak and crack before it broke away from its foundations and tumbled over.

Petrified they held themselves tightly, cradled together against the small wall of dead shufflers which began to shake. Ben lifted his head up just in time to see the zombie pile collapse, trapping them under a coat of rotting corpses.

Zombies surrounded, walking both sides and some even clambering over but Ben, Chris and Ricky were hidden. The dead could not see nor smell the three men.

With no sign of lunch, the large gathering of zombies slowly disbanded, moving away to wander Runcorn Old Town and the bus station close by.

Underneath the decaying dead, Chris whispered to Ben, "Let's make a move."

Ben nodded in agreement and turned his head to locate Ricky, expecting to see his face. He was disgusted to see that next to him was Ricky's bare bottom; his polka dot dress having once again rucked up above his waist.

"Ricky, shift your arse out of my face will you, it smells worse that the dead bloke on top of me. Ricky!" Ben moaned.

"No, I'm staying right here. There's zombies everywhere and I'm not moving till they've all gone!" Ricky replied.

Ben shifted his eyes and saw a zombie hand resting close by. Managing to free his right arm, he grabbed the hand and shoved a rigid index finger up Ricky's bottom, making his friend leap from beneath the heap of bodies.

"Fuck me Ben, you sicko. The only finger allowed up there is mine!" He yelled.

Every zombie close by was alerted to Ricky's presence and they started to shuffle his way.

Chris and Ben freed themselves from under the zombie mound and stood up. The three of them looked for a route of escape but zombies approached from every direction. There was no clear exit, not without fighting their way out. Then they heard vehicles approaching; the rumbling of motorbike engines accompanied by screams of excitement.

In the near distance the vehicles responsible became visible as they headed their way. A small convoy of motorbikes.

Into the approaching zombies the motorbikes drove, the riders swinging crowbars, knifes, bats and hammers to kill the surrounding undead.

Ricky turned to Chris and Ben "We're saved," he smiled, then a crowbar connected with his head, breaking his skull in two.

Chris was next; a hammer to his face split his nose in two and propelled him through the air. Lifting his bloodied face the last thing he saw was the front wheel of a motorbike as it drove over his head.

Both bikes now circled Ben, his dead band mates lay either side of him.

"Why?" he asked.

"Because we can!" replied one of the bikers then they all attacked.

First the hammer bashed into Ben's face, breaking his jaw, sending teeth flying from his mouth. Then a knife stabbed into his stomach. It was a crowbar that finished the job, connecting with his neck, crushing his wind pipe.

The bikers laughed and cheered with bloodlust as Ben choked to death.

Journal Entry 18

Sleep did not find me easily that night. It was extremely dark in Brittain's living room with the only light coming from Butty twitching open the curtains every now and again to check for zombies. My lack of vision seemed to heighten my other senses and the muffled conversation between 80s Dave and Brittain coming from the kitchen was keeping me awake.

I could hear clanging of glasses and drunken blabbering's from Dave. Having found Brittain's booze he had decided to get well and truly oiled and had taken it upon himself to try and cure our host of his agoraphobia.

"Listen Kid, this agoraphobia, it's all in your head. You sit at home watching the news and it's all doom and gloom. Murder, rape, robberies, terrorist attacks... and with modern technology there's barely any reason to leave the house at all. I'm sure you've been living quite comfortably, Ace. You've had your TV and internet to keep you entertained and I bet you've been ordering your shopping online for a home delivery haven't you? More and more people work from home these days too, have you been doing that? I've got this mate, Kenny his name is. Fat fella with a bald head and a moustache. Always sweating and he snores when he's awake. You know the type. Anyway, he runs a telephone sex line from his home. Big June he calls himself. He has a voice changer program on his computer that he connects to his telephone line which makes him sound like a woman. He makes a fortune talking dirty to perverts all day for £2.50 per minute. If only the sticky palmed wankers knew that Big June was actually Big Kenny and they've been stroking one out whilst he tells them the things he'd like to do to a Jaffa Cake. What I'm trying to say is you're a victim of society Kid but society doesn't exist anymore and your creature comforts are gone. What are you going to do when your food supplies run dry? Or when zombies come crashing through your windows and doors. Are you going to starve yourself or just sit there whilst the dead fucks eat you? Come on Brittain kid, wake up and smell the decay. It's time for you to make a change. There's a world outside your window and it's a world of dread and fear, but it's your world kid and it's yours for the taking!"

You won't believe how long I lay there trying to place where I'd heard, "There's a world outside your window and it's a world of dread and fear". The hours I should have spent sleeping so I would be fresh for another horrific day looking for Emily were instead spent battling with my memory to remember where I had heard those words. By the time I'd remembered it was from the song from Band Aid, I was angrier with Bob Geldof than I was with Dave.

After several hours of muffled conversation and drunken laughter the air fell silent and I finally drifted off to slumber land. Mr Sandman was about to take me away to Never Never Land when a prehistoric growl brought me back to life with a start and I stumbled around in the dark attempting to find a weapon. Before I could ask Butty what it was I heard it happen again, rumbling through the floor and up my feet making my legs vibrate.

"Relax John, it's nothing to worry about. It's Oliver Reed next door. Have you never heard a drunk man snoring before?" Butty said, parting the curtains to peep outside.

"That's Dave?" I replied in shock, the walls trembling as he snorted out another deafening snore, "I can't sleep with that going on. I'll have to wake him up."

"No point little brother. You'd have a better chance waking a sedated elephant and even if you did he'd probably go straight back off and start snoring again. Just close your eyes. You'll soon get used to the noise," he suggested.

Well I tried to block it out but it was impossible. Every snort and grunt made my brain rattle. Dave's snoring was relentless and what made it worse was Butty didn't seem to care, he just sat in the window all night keeping look out, occasionally moaning that my restlessness was breaking his concentration.

As soon as the morning broke I decided to wake the fucker up. We had to make up lost ground and I was damned if Dave was going to sleep off his hangover. If I was awake then so was Sleepy Beauty!

I stormed into the kitchen to find Dave, wearing sunglasses and sat on a chair with his head resting on a table, a cigarette hanging out of his mouth. Over his ears were his ever present headphones. Snoring his frigging head off!

"Dave!" I yelled, slamming my fist down on the table for added volume.

To my surprise, Dave woke up instantly and like a reflex, lit the cigarette and began smoking.

"Morning Ace! What time is it? Are we off to find Emily?" he said, with a chipper tone.

Incredible. One night's heavy drinking with only a few hours sleep and he's as right as rain, ready to face the world. I could kill him sometimes.

"How are you not feeling like shit? There's a near empty bottle of whisky next to you and you've only had about four hours sleep. Why are you not hungover? I'm sober as a judge but due to your horrendous snoring my head is banging like I've been on an all-day drinking session with Ozzy Osbourne!" I moaned.

"I never get hangovers John, it's just another reason why I'm so fucking awesome. Speaking of awesome, I was having a brilliant dream till you woke me up. I was at one of those conventions where you get to meet famous people. It was called 'Totally 80s' and every actor and musician that made that decade great were in attendance. I was in heaven Ace, that was until zombies turned up then things went from great to fucking spectacular!" he beamed.

I had no interest what so ever in hearing Dave's dream but he was intent on describing it to me and I was too tired to protest. Plus I figured I might as well get it out of the way now or I'll be getting sound bites about it all bloody day!

"So, I had just left the house to go to work and for some reason I lived next door to BJ & J Owen's Newsagents and I decided to pay Barry's a visit to buy a few packs of tabs, when I saw a flyer on the door for something called 'Totally 80s: The Ultimate 80s Convention'. Now people say that smoking heavily can make you impotent but right there and then I had a chubby the size of a fucking moon rocket. There were people down the other end of the street using it to limbo dance kid. There was no chance I was going to work that day!"

"Oh yeah, my dream took place before the apocalypse so there were no zombies shuffling about. Just the normal brain dead useless cunts we all knew and hated."

"After buying my tabs from Bazza, because even the allure of meeting my heroes does not get in the way of me and my smokes, I left the shop to find that I was no longer on Balfour Street but inside a huge exhibition hall. I mean this place was big Ace. Imagine the space between your ears and times that by one hundred. That's how big this hall was and it was decorated with 80s movie posters and memorabilia but for some reason known only to my brain, greeting me at the front of the hall, was a 20ft statue of Tina Turner and she was mid dance whilst screaming down a microphone. You know the dance move kid. That one where she walks around like she's shit herself and is desperately looking for a toilet. But that wasn't the weird part. The strange thing was that every couple of seconds, Tina would fart and a packet of Benson & Hedges shot out of her arsehole. Also she wasn't wearing any knickers and instead of pubic hair she had dry roasted peanuts. Now I'm no dream analyst and for the life of me I don't know why she was parping out tabs. But I can only assume that Tina's peanut thatch had something to do with Nutbush City Limits. It is her best song after all."

"I walked through Tina's legs and entered the main area, pocketing a few packs of B&H as a windy gust fired them out of her Golden Eye. I couldn't believe my eyes. Movie and music stars filled the arena and I was the only average Joe there. To my left, Mike Score who is the lead singer with Flock of Seagulls was asking Jermaine Stewart if he could borrow some mousse for his hair as it had lost

94

all of its bounce and was getting in his eyes. Jermaine didn't have any though. He was busy drinking cherry wine whilst stalking Madonna, telling her to put some clothes on. I had a quiet chat with Mike Score and told him he was barking up the wrong tree with Jermaine and if it was hair product he was after then he needs to talk to Bonnie Tyler who was getting pissed at the bar with the cast from Time Bandits."

"Everywhere I looked I saw more and more famous people, all mingling with each other and the best thing of all was they had time for me and had no problems answering all of my questions. For instance, did you know that Chuck Norris' beard has its own agent and actually earns more money that he does? Me neither! And that Belinda Carlisle was actually born in Carlisle and her hair is made from Shredded Wheat? It's true! She told me in my dream. Whenever she wants a haircut she washes her hair in milk and hires a group of small children to eat it."

"I was having a great time, shooting the shit with the stars then all of a sudden a fuck off siren sounded and Martin Kemp from Spandau Ballet, who up to this point had been swapping make up tips with Steve Strange from Visage, told me that it meant the public were about to come in. I was fucking gutted, lar. There I was hob knobbing with the stars from the greatest decade of all time and now I had to share them with the great unwashed. "I think George Michael must have sensed my upset as he offered me a joint but I punched the greasy bastard in the face and told him to do one."

"Everyone took seats behind tables and sat awaiting their public but it wasn't the public that arrived. It was zombies, hundreds of them! They weren't like real zombies either John, these were fast fuckers!

In they came in there droves running towards us and they were hungry."

"The first to be eaten was Mike Score. He couldn't see a thing with his hair flopping over his eyes and ended up tripping over the bike from the TV show Streethawk, falling flat on his face. He was easy pickings for the undead. "

"Celebrities were dropping like flies and I was getting angry John, real fucking angry! Zombies were destroying everything that was awesome about the 80s and I had to make a stand and fight back."

"Catch!" Came a voice to my right. I turned to see Robert Englund dressed as Freddy Krueger and he threw me my Battle Paddle. "You're all my children now!" he shouted, slicing off the heads of approaching zombies with his metal claw glove."

"Nice one Krueger lad!" I yelled with appreciation. Then I began thwarting all oncomers. Twatting them with my awesome Battle Paddle. But it was hard going and no matter how many zombies I killed they kept on coming, making it impossible for me to save anyone."

"Then out of nowhere Michael Dudikoff, star of the American Ninja films, jumped over my head and launched hundreds of ninja stars, one by one towards the zombies. Every star thrown hit its target, piercing through the skull and into the brain of every deader. With Freddy Krueger and Dudikoff on my side we were turning the fight around and the approaching zombies became less and less."

"Finally the onslaught of the undead waned and the three of us stood victorious. I offered Michael Dudikoff my hand to say thanks and like a true Ninja he disappeared in a puff of smoke. I couldn't see Freddy Krueger at first but then I found him murdering Brother Beyond and The Kids from Fame even though they weren't even zombies! 'Fair enough' I thought, and so I left him to his rampage."

"Now the zombies were taken care of I was hoping things would get back to normal and I could continue talking bollocks with my new celebrity mates but all was not well. Most of those that had survived the attack were now looking rather ill and began collapsing. First to go down was Molly Ringwald, followed by the Orang-utan from Any Which Way But Loose and then Steve Guttenberg who had been doing a terrible job of chatting up Blanche from the Golden Girls. I thought Limahl was going to be next to turn green but he was just upset because he had come runner up in a Limahl lookalike competition to a toilet brush, and won one of his singles as a prize!"

"I had my suspicions as to what was making everyone sick so I got Leonard "Bones" McCoy from Star Trek to use his Medical Tricorder and he confirmed my fears. They had all been infected. One by one famous faces from the 1980s were turning into the undead. Unlike the rotters me and my mates Freddy and Dudikoff had taken care of, these were not your fast Hollywood zombies but you're everyday shufflers. This meant killing them should not have been as difficult kidda but I was finding it a struggle. You know me Ace, I love killing zombies but when you're face to face with an undead Roger Moore it's not so easy.

"After reluctantly twatting Roger's head in with the Battle Paddle I looked around to see if apart from me, there was anyone else still alive. Freddy Krueger was OK but he'd gone completely wacko and was riding around on the pantomime horse from Rentaghost like he was king of the rodeo. The only other person I could see that wasn't infected was Boy George but I decided to kill him anyway because he's a massive twat.

"So I lit up one of Tina Turner's arse fags and with my Battle Paddle I started bashing heads.

"WHALLOP! Down went John Cusack like a sack of shit. "That's for making 2012!" I yelled.

"THWACK! To the floor crashed Joe Dolce. Now if you don't remember who Joe Dolce is Ace, he's the annoying prick that pretended to be Italian and sang 'Shaddap You Face', which stopped Vienna by Ultralox getting to the No 1 spot back in 1981. I went into overkill on little Joe Dolce if I'm honest. By the time I had finished his face looked like a rhubarb crumble.

"BAM! On the ground went Andrew McCarthy. "That's for Weekend at Bernie's 2 and for every movie from 1989 onwards," I screamed.

"On and on the zombie bashing continued until every famous face from the 1980s was dead accept for one. Stood beneath the legs of Tina Turner was zombie Gary Numan. Man I just couldn't do it. There was no way I could take him down, I loved the guy too much. Then I heard Tina's belly growl and what followed was the biggest fart I have ever heard and her arse dispatched dozens of cigarettes, hurtling them downwards towards Numan at a record breaking speed. He looked like a porcupine when it was all over.

"So there I stood, surrounded by my heroes and every last one of them was dead when the 20ft statue of Tina Turner came to life, handing me a pint of lager and started singing Simply the Best. It was beautiful Ace and she even let me munch a few of her dry roasted peanut pubes. That's when you woke me up!"

After describing his elaborate and nonsensical dream he lit a cigarette and lent back on his chair with his arms behind his head, waiting on my response. I couldn't think of anything to say! His description had sent my brain to mush and it was difficult to find words. I mean, really? A 20ft Tina Turner with a nutty trouser garden and a cigarette dispenser for an arse? Who thinks of things like that? Dave that's who!

"Wow! I have no idea what I just heard but if I was your psychiatrist I'm pretty sure I'd be calling the men in white coats to come and take you away right about now!" I said, finally summoning a response.

Dave let out an enormous belly laugh at my suggestion then sucked down hard on his cigarette, rocking back and forth on the dining table chair.

"You only got a little snippet there Kid. You want to try living with my brain 24/7. It's not all cheese and biscuits being as cool as me you know!" he replied, pouring himself a large whisky.

"I do have to live with your brain 24/7, you never bloody shut up! If you're not talking about the 1980's then it's some other random nonsense. What was it you were saying the other day? Why in Star Wars does everyone only have one set of clothes and who brushes Chewbacca's fur? Is it Han Solo? And when he brushes his tummy does Chewy kick his leg out like a dog getting a belly rub?" I recalled.

"I've been thinking about those Star Wars questions and I think I've found the answers. There's a washer dryer on the Millennium Falcon and Chewy brushes his own hair using a comb fashioned from the shell of a Felucian ground beetle and the toe nails from a Kowakian Monkey Lizard." Dave smiled, downing his whisky in one.

"Where do you come up with this stuff?" I asked, exasperated.

"What can I say, I'm a fucking genius!" came the expected reply.

Butty walked into the kitchen, grabbed an empty glass and helped himself to a whisky, taking a seat next to Dave at the table.

"He's right about the Millennium Falcon. I've discussed this at length with my comrades from Aliens of Runcorn Spotters Elite. Not only would there be a washer dryer on board, they would also have an iron because none of their clothes were ever creased." Butty said.

"It's the end of the world and I'm surrounded by Star Wars nerds! I see you're both having a healthy breakfast. You should go easy on the whisky, I'm sure our host wouldn't appreciate you drinking it all. Where is Brittain anyway?" I replied.

"Dunno John. The last thing I remember is trying to help him get over his agoraphobia then I passed out bladdered." he said, pouring another drink.

"He's stood outside the front door muttering to himself. He's been there for hours," Butty casually informed.

"He's outside? Butty you've been keeping watch all night and you didn't think this was something you needed to tell us about?" I yelled, running to the front door.

I opened the door to see Brittain stood on his driveway with a zombie closing in, only moments away from grabbing him. Hearing the door open he turned his head to look at me. Track lines from dried out tears ran down his cheeks.

"I'm outside," he shivered and a small smile of accomplishment spread across his face, "I think I'm cured!"

In that moment he looked vibrant. Fresh air hitting his skin for the very first time made him appear more alive than anyone I had ever seen before and what's more, he looked content and happy; far removed from the twitching nervous wreck we had encountered the night before. Then all that was taken away as the oncoming zombie pulled him to the ground and began gnawing at his neck.

I ran towards the kid and grabbing the zombie by its hair, wrenched it away from him, throwing the zombie to the ground. Whilst I returned to Brittain, Butty ran to the zombie and jumping into the air, stomped his boot down hard into its face, cracking the deader's skull. Unfortunately it was too late for Brittain. Not only was he infected but the amount of blood he was losing indicated his passing would be sooner rather than later.

I ripped some material from the ragged shirt of the zombie and pushed it against the kid's neck in an attempt to ease the blood pumping out. Not that it did any good. Nothing was going to save him, we all knew it but I felt like I needed to do something. Holding the material against his neck I spoke softly, reassuring him that everything was going to be OK.

In his final moments Brittain appeared happy, despite the pain he must have felt. I guess that even though he knew his life was about to end, he'd done something he had never before thought possible. He'd stepped out of his home and ventured into the world for the very first time. It was just a shame he hadn't experienced this sooner. Who would have thought that advice from a pissed up 80s Dave could cure agoraphobia? Not Dave that's for sure or I can guarantee he would have kept his massive gob shut!

It didn't take long for him to die. The injury to his neck was substantial and took him much sooner than the infection would have. The last thing Brittain did before breathing his final breath was look at me with the most fulfilled expression I have ever seen. Then a crowbar flew downwards past my face, smashing into the kid's head.

"Time to move," Butty instructed.

This was the second time in a few days that we had met someone and they had died as a consequence. Firstly there was Rod in the medical centre and now this poor kid. Add what had happened to Jonathon and I was starting to think we were jinxed!

"The less people we talk to the better, everyone we meet ends up dead," I groaned.

We heard a loud yawn and behind us in the doorway of the house was Steven, stretching his arms out in an attempt to wake himself up.

"What did I miss?" he asked.

Butty and Dave looked at each other with a similar expression. I knew what they were thinking because I was thinking it too. They do say these things come in threes!

"Two tins of spam says he won't make it through the day," Butty wagered to which Dave keenly accepted.

There was an ear piercing screech, like metal scraping against the ground slowly. We looked down the road to where the cul-de-sac opened into a larger street and saw Dave's Thunderbird bang and clang its way along the road followed by a small horde of zombies.

"Fuck me lar, someone's half inched me Thunderbird and they are driving it with flat tyres! It will destroy the body work! That car is a thing of beauty, what the hell are they thinking?" Dave exclaimed running to the Volvo.

"Do you think its Emily, should we follow?" I asked Butty,

"It could be our Emily, it's definitely worth a shot. We'll keep a good distance between our vehicles and the zombies following the Thunderbird. They are obviously attracted to the noise. There's no point in distracting them, not yet anyway. Not unless we're clear its Emily driving. Did you hear that Dave? Keep your distance!" Butty yelled.

We climbed into our vehicles leaving Brittain's body in his driveway. I liked him, he was a good kid that did not deserve to go out the way he did. But in this post-apocalyptic world people don't always get what they deserve. They get what they take. Only the ruthless survive now and Brittain, with all of his fears and hang ups was not cut out to survive. Or maybe it's our fault he's dead and if we'd picked another house last night he would have found a way to live through this. Happy in his own little world, never really knowing the dangers that lived outside his doorway.

Or maybe I'm over thinking it and it's his own fault for listening to 80s Dave!

Emily 2

Emily was cold and tired. She had been on the move for several hours now but with darkness drawing closer she remembered her uncle's apocalypse training and knew she needed to find somewhere safe to stay for the night.

"Now then Emily love, in the event of a zombie apocalypse there will come a time when you find yourself on the streets looking for a safe place to stay. There are a few rules you will need to follow.

1: Always find somewhere before it goes dark. It will be dangerous enough in the daylight but being outside at night will be suicide. The last thing you want is a zombie creeping up on you when you're struggling to see your own hands in front of your face. Now you may think you would be able to smell them coming and in some cases this could be true but you have to remember that the streets are infested with the dead. Everywhere will smell like death so sniffing out a single rotter could be difficult. It will be like sniffing out a singular fart at a baked bean eating contest.

2: Do not look for refuge in a boarded up house. They are boarded up for a reason and will no doubt contain other survivors that may not be so pleased to see you. Remember, the apocalypse favours crazy bastard arseholes that are willing to do anything to survive. When the end of the world arrives, nice guys will be zombie fodder. Luckily for you, you've got Uncle Butty here to show the way and I'm nuttier than squirrel shit!

3: Once you have found somewhere to stay you need to secure it the best you can. Furniture such as wardrobes and beds are great to push up against doors and windows. Another tip would be to scatter empty tins, cans or pots and pans around entrances and exits. If a zombie or a survivor gets in whilst you are sleeping, the clatter and banging as they walk into them will wake you up."

What would she do without her Uncle?

To Emily's left, a little further along the road, was an apartment with its door open. She smiled and said a silent thank you to her uncle then slowly approached the doorway with caution. The lock had been forced and the hallway leading to a short staircase was empty.

Slowly she entered and holding her hammer tightly she quietly climbed the staircase. At the top she was met with another open door leading to another hallway with two closed doors on either side and another one directly in front which was open. The open door revealed a cosy living room filled with 1970s furniture and a shag pile carpet.

The closer she moved towards the doorway the stronger the smell of death became and entering the living room, she was confronted with the cause of the putrid stench. An old lady sat dead in a chair with a small circular wound to her forehead.

Emily looked over the bloated lady. The women's eyes were bulging out of their sockets and her skin appeared almost purple as the bacteria within began breaking down her body, releasing gases that caused the disgusting smell.

The apartment was perfect for Emily but the old lady would have to be removed. There was not a chance she could rest with the smell of a decomposing body attacking her nostrils.

Emily entered her deceased host's bedroom and retrieved a bed sheet then lay it on the floor in the living room. She then tipped the chair forward and the old lady slid out of her seat and onto the sheet. Wrapping her up and taking the body in her arms, Emily carried her out into the hallway and down the staircase, placing her on the ground outside. She then re-entered the bedroom and rocked a large wardrobe into the hallway and down the stairway, using it to secure the front door. It was difficult but with her uncle's advice in her thoughts she was determined.

Entering the kitchen she emptied the contents of the rubbish bin on the floor. Not one empty tin was found. The old lady's cupboards however were full with cans of rice pudding. Emily hated rice pudding. The slimy texture, the creamy sweet taste; she hated everything about it. Her hatred for rice pudding was on par with her father's dislike of mayonnaise and for a moment he entered her thoughts, she felt sad. Sad that she wasn't with him and for the distress her disappearance will have caused.

"I'll see you soon dad, I got something I need to do first but we'll be together, I promise," she said to herself.

Despite her hatred of the stuff, she knew this food from hell was a good source of protein and the tins could be used as an alarm against intruders. She emptied several of the creamy rice puddings into a bowl and scattered the empty tins on the floor at the bottom of the staircase. The contents of the cutlery draw and pots and pans completed the make shift alarm system.

Wrapping herself in a blanket she stood at the apartment window and began to eat the cold rice pudding, struggling to swallow her most unappetising of meals. The sky outside was clear and the moon illuminated her view. In the near distance she could see the fields of the Pavilions and the many slayed zombies that carpeted the frosty grass. Her first thought was how, with the butchered dead surrounding the grounds, the Pavilions would make the perfect hide out. The smell from the dead would keep zombies away and nobody in their right minds would think about entering. It was truly horrifying.

"Nobody in their right minds..." She said, a thought igniting.

Finishing her meal she turned from the window and curled up on the floor wrapping herself tightly in the blanket. She knew that if she was to avenge Jonathon then she needed to keep her strength up and a good night's rest was a necessity. Besides, she wanted to be fresh and alert when she investigated the Pavilions in the morning.

Closing her eyes she quickly fell into a deep sleep, exhausted after a long couple of days.

It was early morning when she woke. The rumbling of a car engine approaching and the banging, clanging and scraping that came with it wakened her from her slumber. Emily couldn't believe her eyes as 80s Dave's Ford Thunderbird struggled towards her location, a large gathering of zombies following behind. Her first thoughts were to hide, believing her father, Dave and Uncle Butty had caught up with her but on closer inspection she noticed that her family were not in the vehicle.

She watched as the Thunderbird stalled directly outside the apartment before becoming surrounded by zombies. Inside the vehicle she saw a tall thin man with long black hair and a young girl sobbing whilst cradling a screaming baby.

"Fuck!"

Journal Entry 19

We trailed the screeching Thunderbird whilst being careful to keep a safe distance between our vehicles and the horde of rotters ahead of us. The clanging, banging and scraping as the car struggled forward on four flat tyres was so loud it echoed throughout Weston Point, attracting every zombie in the area. My mind, or what little remained of it, was a complete mess. If it was Emily driving how the hell were we going to save her? Four men with a selection of crowbars, a cricket bat and a large mayonnaise stirring spoon against what must have been over one hundred zombies and counting? Even Butty was looking nervous; driving whilst chewing his lip and tapping his fingers against the steering wheel.

Dave was ahead of us, setting the slow pace in his Volvo with Steven sat in the back seat. I could see Dave's head bobbing up and down and his left arm making exaggerated movements. He would angrily fist pump the air occasionally with his brown leather driving glove attired hand. Anyone would have thought both he and Steven were having a heated argument but I knew better. He was listening to some inspirational 80s tunes, getting himself into the fighting spirit. Most probably Kung Fu Fighting, Eye of the Tiger or anything by Culture Club because as Dave always says…

"Nothing makes me want to rip off someone's head and shit down their necks more than listening to that hedonistic gob shite, Boy George!"

Every few minutes Steven turned his head to look at Butty and I. He looked terrified, like an innocent man on Death Row being led to the electric chair. His face presented an expression that said "Are we really doing this? There's too many of them! What the hell are you guys thinking? I didn't sign up for this! I want to live not die! Get me out of this car and away from this Scouse maniac!"

Keeping our distance we continued, slowly chugging along trying not to grab any undead attention. The amount of zombies made it difficult to see where one road ended and another began. It was like following a large protest march and to help take my mind off the possibility of Emily leading the horde, I imagined the zombies shuffling along with large placards brandishing slogans such as "Zombies have rights too!", "Dead and unfed!" and "Stop the rot!"

My silly musing did little to ease my stress and the concern on my brother's face was not doing anything to help!

"You look worried Butty, I'm not used to seeing you like this," I frowned. "The last time I saw you this nervous was just before you asked Sharon Grimshaw out on a date. That didn't end too well from what I can remember. What was it she said? "Fuck off you mentalist"?

"Something like that. More fool her because if she had said yes then maybe she would be alive now instead of decomposing in my back garden with the other zombies I killed," he replied with just the smallest hint of a smile.

"What's the plan? Please tell me you've thought up a plan because at this point all I've got is run at them with a crowbar and hope for the best." I asked.

"Well I've been thinking. All we've got tying Emily to the car is that it's Dave's Thunderbird," Butty said, spitting out a freshly bitten nail from his finger. "We have no other reason to suspect she would be driving it. But we have been searching for her since yesterday morning and so far, this is the only lead we've had. Now my instinct is telling me that she's not driving. I have to ask myself what I would do and there is no way I would drive a car with flat tyres and create that amount of noise. You might as well be ringing a bell whilst shouting "eat me!" The problem is that due to the amount of zombies following the car, we cannot say for sure if Emily is in there and although my instinct says she isn't, there is reasonable doubt. Which means only one thing, we're going to have to take the dead bastards out and you're not far off with running at them with a crowbar but only after we've run as many of them over as we can. I'm not convinced Dave's Volvo is up to the job but this Land Rover should take care of a lot of them. Even if the impact doesn't kill them it will snap a few limbs, make them less of a threat. My bigger concern is where we are. You remember The Pavilions don't you? How many zombies you saw heading towards it? Well it's just up ahead and if we're going to make our move, we're best doing it soon before we get there and we end up faced with an army to deal with."

We turned on to the bottom of Sandy Lane, a long ascending road which contained the entrance to The Pavilions. At the speed we were moving we were still a good distance away from reaching the grounds of the large social club but Butty was right. If we were going to act it would have to be fast. Then Dave brought his Volvo to a halt and held his hand out of the window instructing us to stop also. It wasn't clear why at first then we realised the horde of zombies had stopped moving. We all left our vehicles and grouped together.

"Whoever is driving my Thunderbird must have stopped, which means they are either trapped inside or they've made a run for it. If we're going to do this now is the time kidda,"Dave said, cracking his knuckles and gearing himself up for a fight.

"I have to, it could be Emily and I can't take the risk that it isn't. I'd never forgive myself," I quivered, my body shaking with nerves and adrenaline.

"Well we're with you kid, let's go and fuck up some dead cunts!" Dave smiled whilst placing his arm around a petrified Steven.

"John and I will go first and clear as many with the Land Rover as we can. You and Steven follow but be careful, don't drive in too deep. Hit, reverse, repeat. Hit, reverse, repeat." Butty explained.

The noise of an approaching vehicle could be heard and we all turned to see a red Mini Cooper speeding to our location. As well as the noise from its engine the car stereo could be heard blasting out the Superman theme tune.

We dove for cover as the Mini Cooper hurtled towards the zombie horde up ahead with what looked like a big green hand sticking out of the window.

"Maybe I'm losing my mind but did anyone else just see the Incredible Hulk driving a Mini?" I asked.

"It looked like a Teenage Mutant Ninja Turtle to me!" Steven replied, scratching his head.

"I don't know who it was Ace but I'm sure they were wearing a cape." Dave responded.

We watched the Mini speed forward and smash into the zombie horde before reversing back and pulling up beside us. The driver window lowered to reveal a masked women starring back me. She was wearing a Star Trek uniform, Superman cape and had a large plastic Hulk fist on her hand. On the passenger seat next to her I saw a Klingon Bat'leth and I spied a broadsword and Lightsaber in the back.

"When you lot have finished gawping you might want to get in your vehicles and give me a hand, or is zombie killing women's work these days?" She said, before speeding away towards the horde again.

"You heard the girl, let's kill some zombies!" Butty roared with renewed fire in his Belly.

We got back in our vehicles and started the engines, watching as the Mini Cooper again struck the large gathering of shufflers before reversing all the way back to our location.

She lifted her head out of the window and yelled "I love the smell of zombies in the morning!" then accelerated away again!

"Who is that girl?" I asked.

"I don't know but I think I'm in love!" Butty replied.

Butty put his foot down and we sped towards the zombies. I tried keeping my eyes open at first but the closer we got the more terrified I became. So crunching my eyelids closed I pushed myself back into the seat and prepared the best I could for impact. When the collision came it was as hard as I had expected and an airbag expanded into my face restricted my vision but the moans... my god the noise of the undead was deafening. I was only glad I was wearing my seat belt or the force may have sent me through the windscreen! Butty quickly put the car in reverse and we were out of the chaos as quickly as we had ploughed into it.

Bringing the car to a halt, Butty pulled out a knife and stabbed at the airbag, restoring my vision just in time to see Dave's Volvo crash into the zombies and crash it did! Smoke bellowed into the air and the bonnet flew up. Dave and Steven were in trouble.

We shot forward again and rammed into the zombies grabbing at the right of Dave's Volvo. The mysterious girl in the Mini did the same and smashed into the zombies to the Volvo's left. I looked to the vehicle to see Dave and Steven kicking at the windscreen to escape.

We moved out once again. Hit, reverse, repeat was the order of the day. Hammering back into the undead, we saw that Dave and Steven had successfully removed the windscreen and were now on top of the Volvo; Steven frantically kicking at reaching zombies and Dave whacking anything that came close with his Battle Paddle. But they were quickly becoming overwhelmed. Sure Butty and the masked girl in the Mini were effectively clearing zombies from the sides but to the front they clambered forward, falling into each other. It was only the raised bonnet which was stopping the dead from clawing their way onto the vehicle.

"Both of you jump over, you're going to die if you don't!" I yelled.

Dave jumped from the roof of the Volvo to that of our land Rover then yelled for Steven to follow. Readying himself to leap over, a zombie grabbed Steven's ankle and he tripped, smashing his face into the roof of the car.

"Stevo get up off your fucking arse now! Nobody else is dying today!" Dave shouted, spearing the Battle Paddle at the many undead trying to grab at him.

Steven was dazed by the fall and before he knew what was happening, the zombie that had grabbed at his ankle pulled him off the roof and into the horde. Every zombie close by tugged and yanked and ripped into his flesh, pulling him apart like pulled pork.

Amongst his screams the last thing I heard him yell was "I'm coming Jess! I'm coming!"

"Hold on Dave!" Butty shouted before pulling the Land Rover back into reverse and quickly retreating.

Once at a safe distance Dave climbed down from the roof and into the back of the car.

"Fuck me lar, that's two people dead already this morning and I've only been awake an hour! You pair better not die on me. I'm starting to get a complex here!" he said.

I looked ahead to see the Mini Cooper hurtle into more zombies. The hit and run method was working and the large gathering of deaders was gradually lessening. There was now just as many squirming on the ground as there was on their feet and more importantly we could now see the Thunderbird. From the amount of zombies pounding on it, the driver was still inside.

Butty put his foot on the throttle and we continued to run over as many zombies as we could. Smash after smash we drove into the horde, slowly but surely knocking them to the ground. As the numbers of those knocked down increased, the task changed from running them over to rolling back and forth over their fallen bodies, squishing as many rotting heads as we could. The amount of mashed limbs and splattered bodies wasn't making it easy. It was like driving through heavy mud and it didn't take long for both ours and the masked girl's vehicle to become stuck, trapped in a thick layer of tangled limbs.

Not too far away was the Thunderbird and roughly forty or so zombies that we had so far been unable to attack. With the cars immobile, we were going to have to get our hands dirty to finish the job.

Dave sparked a cigarette, pushed open the car door and leaped out of the back of the vehicle, thrusting the Battle Paddle into the heads of any zombies squirming on the floor. There was a rage burning inside of him that was clear to see. He had a lot of aggression to work out following the death of Steven and before him, Brittain. It was a good job he had a lot of dead people to take it out on!

Butty and I followed, bashed anything that moved. Man it was slow and difficult work. Not only from drilling our weapons into the heads of the fallen but from walking across the carpet of twisted and bloodied limbs beneath us. Every step landed on a slippery leg, a busted open chest, a contorted arm or a splattered face. It was disgusting and tiresome but each step took us closer to the Thunderbird.

Ahead of us was the masked girl, stomping on zombie heads with her Dr Martens boots, smashing them with her hulk fist and slicing them open with her Klingon Bat'leth. She was fierce and relentless in her attacks, yelling "DIE BASTARD DIE!" every time she killed one. If I'm honest she scared the shit out of me but for some reason she had taken it upon herself to join our fight and to her credit, she was killing a lot more of the deaders than we were!

After the disgusting and hideous journey across the road of twisted limbs we caught up with the masked girl. Greeting us now was the gathering of zombies shuffling around the Thunderbird.

"Why are you helping us?" I asked the girl.

"I'm not, I'm helping myself," she replied, marching forward to attack the dead.

Well I had no idea what she meant by that, I was just glad to have someone as kick ass as her on our team!

We followed her into the fight, belting anything and everything in the head that came close enough. What was apparent quite quickly was the lack of attack from the zombies. They only appeared interested in us when we got up close and personal. It appears the sheer number of rotting corpses was hindering their sense of smell and only when we were right under their noses did they react. By that point it was too late. Whollop! A hard strike to the head and they were down.

Several minutes of zombie bashing later and we were close to the Thunderbird. My heart was racing as I thwacked and cracked my way through the small horde.

Removing a dead zombie that was slumped against the driver's window, I peered inside. The glass was coated with blood making it difficult to see. All I could make out was the outline of a figure stooped over the wheel. I tried the door handle but it was locked.

"Emily!" I cried, rubbing the sleeve of my jacket against the glass to remove the thick covering of plasma.

A few swift wipes with my sleeve and a small clearing was made, large enough for me to see inside. I placed my eyes to the glass to see a man staring back at me.

"It's not her, it's not Emily!" I cried, falling to my knees, sobbing freely.

Everything we had just been through and it wasn't her. Steven had lost his life and for what? So we could save some guy that had been stupid enough to steal a car and drive it with four flat tyres attracting every zombie in Runcorn. I was so upset it took a while for me to realise Butty had been calling my name.

"John! John! Stop crying you soft shit and look, she's here! Emily is here!"

I couldn't believe it, there she was! A bloodied hammer by her side and a collection of dead zombies at her feet.

I ran to her, clambering over the fallen zombies to fling my arms around her tightly. Emily wept. Shit, we both did! We had both been through so much it was an emotional reunion. After a few moments of blubbering she looked me in the eye and said she was sorry for leaving and asked for my forgiveness. But there was nothing for me to forgive. If anything she should be forgiving me! I should never have tried to keep things from her. To think that leaving her with Barry was the right thing to do was a terrible idea. She wanted revenge for what happened to Jonathon and her uncle's house. So did we and if we were to be successful we needed to stick together.

"None of this is your fault, it's mine. All I wanted to do was protect you but I ended up pushing you away. We're in this together, we all are. Where one goes, we all go. I am never losing you again," I sobbed.

"I love you Dad," Emily smiled, placing her head on my shoulder.

"Alright then, let's find out who the clown is that thought it was a good idea to drive my vintage wheels on four flat tyres!" Dave huffed, marching towards the Thunderbird.

The driver's door opened and out stepped a tall thin man with long black hair. I could see the anger in Dave, he was ready to burst! Before he could unleash a tirade of abuse at the man for what he had done, one of the rear car doors opened and a young girl holding a baby stepped out.

"It's a good job you've got your kids with you or I may have knocked your head off for what you did to my car. What were you thinking? She's ruined! "You better pray to Devo that the tape deck still works!" Dave complained, a tearful quiver to his voice.

"This is your car? Are you Lone Wolf?" Nick asked excitedly.

"You what? Lone Wolf? John, we've found another crazy bastard!" Dave shouted, walking past the man to inspect the car.

Upon hearing the man say Lone Wolf, Butty pulled his crowbar out of the skull of the last shuffling zombie and walked towards him, slowly; like a cowboy preparing for a shootout.

"I'm Lone Wolf," he scowled in his best Clint Eastwood voice.

"Trust No-one told me that if I needed help, I should track you down. When I found your house burnt out I thought maybe you went down with it. It was starting to go dark and we took shelter in this old thing. We must have fallen asleep and when we woke up we were surrounded by zombies. I had no choice but to drive it away. By the time I'd realised the noise was attracting more of them there was too many. I couldn't have stopped even if I wanted to." Nick replied.

"Where is Trust No-one now?" Butty growled.

"He's dead," came the grave reply.

It was like watching two cowboys having a snarling match before a gun fight I could see the suspicion in my brother's eyes. He was weighing up if he could trust the man or not. Then there was this stranger with the kids, not knowing if Butty was a lunatic or not. It took a few moments to click but then I remembered where I'd heard the name Lone Wolf before. It was my brother's A.R.S.E. handle and Trust No-one was the name of one of his fellow Alien Spotters.

"I've been inside Churchill Mansions since the outbreak. My name is Nick and this is Sophie and the baby is Gaby. I'm their guardian I suppose. Thanks for helping us. I don't know what we would have done if you hadn't have turned up," Nick said, placing his arm around Sophie.

"How did he die?" Butty grunted.

"He was murdered by a crazy old bitch and her son. They got theirs though, I made sure of it." Nick replied with venom.

Butty, having finished weighing up if Nick was a threat or not, changed his approach from moody American cowboy to his regular Runcorn crazy guy character.

"You seem like an OK fella and any friend of Trust No-one's is a friend of mine but I don't think we can help, I'm afraid. My house is gone and we have very limited supplies. Taking into account you and the girls, we've probably only got enough spam to last a couple of days," Butty explained.

"Plus, everyone we meet ends up dead so if I were you I'd scarper now before it's too late kid. You've been in our company for about five minutes already which has probably knocked a significant chunk off your lives. Another five and you'll be living on borrowed time." Dave piped up from inside the Thunderbird.

"Dave's right. We don't have a good track record when it comes to helping people and if you come with us then the only thing I can guarantee is trouble. We're not looking for a safe place at the moment. We're looking for payback! No good will come from being in our company," Butty added.

"There's a place you can stay just over there," Emily said, gesturing towards a small apartment, "It's not the biggest but it can be made secure. I stayed there last night. I'll show you now. I'll be right back Dad, I promise."

Emily took Nick and the kids to the apartment. It's hard to describe how good it was to have her back with me. She is my world and being without her once again has been unbearable. The only thing that kept me from going completely insane was Dave harping on about his obsession with the 1980s and Butty with his unusual but effective apocalypse survival methods. Speaking of the terrible twosome, after Emily had taken Nick and the kids away to the apartment, I noticed the pair were in cahoots, discussing our next move.

"I know it's still morning but as far as today goes, we've seen more action than Katie Price's gynaecologist," Dave so eloquently put.

"There's enough dead zombies out here to hide our scent for a long time. We should join the others in the apartment, rest and decide what we're going to do next. Besides I want to quiz the new bloke a bit more on what happened to my pal in Churchill Man..."

Butty was cut short by the sound of vehicles approaching and in the near distance, at the entrance to the Pavilions, two motorbikes appeared followed by the blue transit van we had been searching for. All three of us dove to the ground, lying face down between the many slaughtered zombies in the hope they wouldn't notice we were alive! Well none of us had washed for a few days (Butty for months probably). Sure we were breathing, but stench wise there wasn't much difference!

I couldn't have chosen my spot to hide any worse if I had tried. In my haste to hide myself I had landed on top of a female zombie, face to face and groin to groin! If she was alive this would have been classed as assault! My head had come down directly on to hers and we were eyes to eye. It would have been eyes to eyes but one of hers was missing and to make things doubly gross, the one eye she did have had popped out of its socket and was resting on her pale rotting cheek!

As the vehicles approached I suddenly remembered the girl in the mask that had helped us to destroy the horde. Where the hell was she? I lifted my head from the zombie woman's face and her eye ball stuck to my cheek! I had a quick look around but I couldn't see her anywhere. I hoped to god she had scarpered and wasn't in view.

"Butty!" I whispered, "The girl with the mini, where is she?"

"Fucked if I know. Keep your head down and shut up!" came the stern reply followed by a quizzical frown as he spied the eyeball stuck to my face!

Swiftly I lowered my head, once again resting face to face with the zombie. I've done some gross things these last few days but this was right up there with the worst of them and to make matters worse, the eye ball that was stuck to my cheek began to move, slowly slipping and sliding its way towards my mouth. But I couldn't move, the vehicles were right upon us and I couldn't risk giving away our presence!

The vehicles pulled up and the rumbling noise from the engines told me they were close. Real close! Then I heard the doors of the van open and people dismount their bikes.

"Do you see all this? Look at them all. They weren't here yesterday, no way. It was pretty clear when we drove through."

"Look at all the bad men Ed, there's zillions of them."

"We should tell Ged right away, he'd want to know about this"

"Why Ed? They're all dead aren't they? They're no threat to us and besides, he's sent us out to get supplies. If we came back so soon he would be pissed and the last thing we want to do is piss him off. We all saw what happened to Paul, I don't want to put my head on Ged's chopping block but if you and Tom feel like it then go ahead. Be my guest. I say we tell him about this when we get back from looting and not before. Besides, the more dead zombies the better right? The smell should keep rotters away for a long time."

"Hey look at these two love birds!"

I felt a heavy boot press down on my arse, pushing my meat and two veg repeatedly into the dead zombie girl's groin area. Oh man it was gross, not only could I feel my bits pressing against her cold dead… ahem… lady garden, but there was a horrible squelching sound accompanying this violation. But what the hell could I do but stay rigid, err I mean stiff, no I mean firm… oh fuck me, pretend to be dead! What could I do but pretend to be a zombie? Any kind of movement from me and the game would be up and I'd have gotten the three of us killed!

"Give it to her big guy. Oh yeah that's right!"

"You're fucking sick …. Funny but sick! Come on we better be moving. Are you two losers coming or are you going to go back and cry to Ged because you're scared of a few dead zombies? I'm sure he'll be happy to see you've made us go look for supplies without your van."

"No, we're coming. But if anything happens I'll make sure he knows this was your call."

The vehicles revved their engines and sped away, bumping and jolting over the fallen zombies. I pulled myself off (stop it) from the female zombie I had just been unintentionally intimate with and was joined by Dave.

"You heartless bastard John! Don't tell me you were just going to walk away without saying goodbye? You could at least left her your number Ace. Look at her, she looks all loved up," Dave smirked as we both looked at the dead girl and her eye that had popped out of its socket; A withered tongue poking out of her pale mouth.

Ignoring Dave I turned to Butty who was staring at the entrance to the Pavilions.

"We've got him John. We've got the bastard!"

Better Off Dead

Runcorn was now a dead town. Streets where residents once lived, parks where children once played and roads that directed traffic were now occupied by the undead, picking at the remains of corpses. Less than a week ago the town had a living population of nearly seventy thousand. Now that number closer represented the volumes of zombies. The living, were sparse and nowhere to be seen.

From behind his wheel, Ed sat rigid and silent, concentrating on the road. He manoeuvred the van, dodging meandering zombies and weaving between crashed and abandoned cars. Every once in a while, he would break concentration and take a brief moment to look at the streets around him, at the town he once loved.

Rain clouds loomed, adding to the harrowing apocalyptic scenery. Ed didn't recognise his town anymore and the feeling of safety and comfort derived from living there was gone. He wanted out, for both himself and for Tom and now that Ged had added to his murderous party with the additions of Billy, Kitty, Johno and Deano, he was convinced that an opportunity to disappear unnoticed was imminent. He believed it wouldn't be too long before they could slip away quietly and escape the company of the psychopaths they had found themselves associated with.

In contrast to Ed's concerted and careful driving, Johno and Deano were reckless; daring each other to purposely drive their motorbikes over the heads of the many dead, hollering and whooping when the skulls of the fallen splattered and cracked under the stress of their heavy wheels.

Tom shuddered and squirmed in his seat, sinking down as low as he could in an attempt to restrict his view from their sick game.

"Just close your eyes Tom, you look ridiculous bending over like that and with the size of you, you're never going to get down low enough. Close your eyes tight, and think about food for a while, maybe think about all the corned beef in the world! It will take your mind of those two lunatics. Plus you're putting me off my driving," Ed said.

Tom sat up straight and squeezed his eyes shut as hard as he could; his face shaking with strain and concentration.

"Corned beef, corned beef, corned beef!" he said to himself over and over.

Ed smiled at his friend before turning his attention back to the road and Johno and Deano, who continued to scream and yell in excitement.

It was going to be a long day's looting!

After what felt like a lifetime they arrived at their destination: Runcorn train station. Outside the station it was relatively clear apart from the corpses of course; they were now a staple of every road in Runcorn. The only things joining them were two taxi cabs, parked next to each other in the rank opposite the station entrance.

The first of the vehicles appeared abandoned but in the driver's seat of the second taxi, sat the driver. A large man, undead and secured by his seatbelt, he was twisting his body towards the door, thrashing to break free whilst gnarling at the window.

Ed pulled over just short of the rank and watched Johno and Deano, slowly circle the two taxis before bringing their bikes to a halt and dismounting. He looked on as they taunted the zombie taxi driver, spitting at the car door window and shouting, "Bite me zombie fuck!", and "How much from here to the Pavilions, zombie cunt?"

"They should just kill the bad man or leave him alone. He can't hurt anyone; he's trapped inside the car so why are they yelling at him?" Tom asked.

"Small things amuse small minds. They'll soon get fed up of teasing him, Tom. Come on, we best get moving and catch them up. Stay close to me at all times," Ed replied, opening the van door.

Johno and Deano, now bored with the zombie in the taxi, had made their way to the railway station entrance where they were joined by Ed and Tom. The entrance comprised of two large glass faced automatic doors.

"I say we throw the fat lad through them," Johno snarled whilst Deano attempted unsuccessfully to lever the doors open with his hands.

Ed, closely followed by Tom moved towards the abandoned taxi and opening the driver's door. He reached under the seat and retrieved a large heavy duty torch. It was big, the size of a police baton and as wide as an axe handle. Without warning to the others he threw it hard towards the glass doors, shattering one of the panels.

Shards of glass shot through the air as Johno and Deano scrambled for cover, diving for safety whilst shielding their faces with raised arms.

"Problem solved," Ed smirked.

"How did you know that was going to be there?" Tom asked confused.

"There's not a taxi driver in this town that doesn't keep something they can use to defend themselves close to hand. Come on. Let's go face the music," Ed smiled, walking Tom towards the others.

"You crazy bastard, we could have been cut to shit!" Deano screamed, storming towards Ed, "You better watch yourself Ed. First you try to turn back when you saw all the dead zombies and now you pull this! You're up to something I know it! Anymore tricks like that and maybe you won't make it back. Maybe we kill you and your fat friend and tell Ged you were eaten by zombies and we couldn't save you, how does that sound eh?"

Ed didn't greet this threat with a reply and instead stood his ground, glaring at him coldly.

The four men stepped through the broken station doors; the sound of shattered glass crunching under their feet as they walked into the ticketing area.

To their right were three Perspex fronted ticketing booths and behind the middle booth, a zombie station worker repetitively slammed into the booth whilst growling hungrily at the four men.

Arrogant and cocksure, Johno and Deano approached the zombie and began teasing it as they did with the taxi driver.

"You hungry boy? Come on, try harder. COME ON!" Johno jeered.

The zombie crashed into the booth, head butting it so hard that its forehead cracked and thick congealed blood smeared against the Perspex glass. The sound made Johno jump back a few spaces before composing himself, then stepping up to the ticketing booth he prodded his finger against the glass where the zombie's forehead was resting.

"Must try harder!" Johno grinned.

He moved away from the zombie and walked towards an automatic ticket machine, rocking it forcefully until it toppled, falling heavily onto its side. Retrieving a crowbar from inside his jacket he pelted the machine several times, smashing the front plastic panels.

"I've got this, you go and see what you can get out of the cash machine", he said to Deano.

Tossing a hammer in his hand Deano ran at the cash machine and attacked it vigorously, smashing the tool into it repeatedly.

Both of them whooped and cheered as they smashed their weapons into the machines, enjoying the destruction.

Ed pulled Tom close, "let's leave those morons to it. The fools still think there is value in money. Follow me, I know where the real bounty is."

Ed led Tom away from the ticketing area, towards the back of the station and a large closed metal shutter.

"Behind there is enough food and water to keep us going for days. And we're going to need it if we're to leave," Ed smiled, placing a hand on the big man's shoulder.

"LEAVE! We're going away? ESCAPING!" Tom said excitedly before Ed quickly hushed him into silence.

"We don't belong with Ged or these guys and now is as good a chance as any. Behind this shutter is the station shop. We'll grab what we can, load the van and make a run for it. Those two idiots will be distracted for a while. For all they know we're loading the van with loot for Ged. We'll be out of here before they've had time to notice," Ed explained.

Ed placed a crowbar inside the bottom left corner of the shutter and pulled, creating a gap big enough for the two men to enter.

Inside the station shop they found the shelves to be fully stocked with confectionary supplies. Chocolates, snack bars, crisps, sweets and a large selection of drinks greeted them. Also welcoming them was a foul, festering stench. Tom pulled his shirt over his nose and squinted his eyes.

"What is that Ed? It smells like the day room of the old people's home where my Grandad lives. It's ruining my appetite!" Tom balked.

Following his nose, Ed located the ready-made food counter, containing rotting beef burgers, hotdogs and mouldy sandwiches. Initially he assumed this to be the source of the smell but approaching the counter he soon found the real cause. Behind the putrid food display, slumped on the floor was a deceased shop assistant. His stomach had been pulled apart and maggots crawled in and out of the open cavity.

For a brief moment Ed gazed at the man, mesmerised by the grotesque sight before him. Then it hit him. Something or someone must have done this to the assistant and whatever it was must still be inside the shop with them. He quickly turned to Tom to see his friend smiling back at him, a mouth full of chocolate.

"Guess what Ed; the smell hasn't stopped me from eating after all!" he beamed.

Behind Tom was an open door giving access to a stock room. Stumbling through the door came the shop manager; drying blood and thick saliva covered her mouth and blouse.

Ed was too far away to stop it and Tom, too preoccupied with food was an easy target for the approaching zombie. The first he knew of the undead manageress's presence was when she chomped into his neck.

"No!" Ed screamed, rushing to help his friend.

Tom shrieked, such was the pain from the zombie gnawing into him. He pushed her away forcefully, sending her crashing into the metal shutters creating a loud 'CLANG!

With tears filling his eyes Tom wailed in pain and anger began to take him. He approached the zombie and punched her hard in the face, busting her nose wide open.

He hit her again. Then again and again and again. His strikes hit with such power that after only a few punches her head was turned into a bloodied and broken mess. The zombie manageress was dead.

During the onslaught, Tom became lost in a violent frenzy and Ed, watching in shock, no longer recognised the friend he had grown to love as a brother. Never in the many years that they had been friends had he known Tom to so much as threaten anyone, never mind strike them. He was the true definition of a gentle giant and this, this was a new side to him that nobody had seen.

Tom stepped back from the dead zombie, collapsed to his knees and placed a bloodied hand over the wound on his neck.

"Am I going to be one of the bad men now Ed? I am aren't I? That's why I lost my temper isn't it. The bad man in me, he's taking over," he whimpered.

Ed knew there was no coming back from this. It was only a matter of time before the infection took Tom and he became one of the living dead. He couldn't let that happen, not to his friend. He couldn't let him turn.

"What the hell is going on back there? You two better... fuck! Oh shit fat boy got bitten. You're infected, hahaha!" yelled Johno, delighted at his discovery as he crawled through the gap in the metal shutters.

"I best kill him now before he turns. That big bastard will be unstoppable as a zombie," he said to Ed, readying his crowbar.

About to swing the crowbar, Johno halted at the last minute as Ed stepped between the two, acting as a barrier to protect his friend.

"You stupid fuck!" Johno growled, then pelted Ed in the side of the head with the crowbar, knocking him out and crashing into the shop shelving.

Johno grinned menacingly and lifted his weapon high then brought it down quick and hard towards Tom's head. But the expected impact of metal against skull never came. Instead the crowbar was met with resistance as Tom's large hand clasped it tightly. Angrily, he rose to his feet.

"I am not a bad man yet!" he growled, yanking the crowbar from Johno's grasp then pushing it hard into the centre of his face, splitting his nose open.

"Look what you've done to my face, I'm going to fucking kill you for this!" he screamed.

Letting go of the crowbar, Tom gripped Johno by his throat, pushing him against the shelving. With his free hand, the big guy reached for nearby confectionary and began forcing it into Johno's mouth. Snickers, Twix, Wispa, Mars Bars, Lion Bars... Tom filled his throat with anything he could grab until there was room for no more.

A groggy Ed came to, opening his eyes to see Tom standing over a dead Johno, choked to death by confectionary.

The metal shutters rattled and Deano crawled through the gap. He looked at Tom stood over Johno and with hammer in hand, dashed towards him. Before he could gain any speed, Tom tackled him at the waist, spearing him into the shutters. The impact was such that the shutters broke away from their frame completely and both men were sent crashing to the station floor.

Deano struggled to his feet. Holding his waist in pain he attempted to make a run for it, waywardly walking through the shattered automatic doors and stumbling towards his motorbike. Tom followed, slowly stalking his prey.

Deano mounted his bike then, noticing Tom was closing in, he panicked and fumbled with his keys, dropping them to the ground.

Bending down to retrieve them he was met with a boot to the face, propelling him from his bike and hitting the road with a thud.

Tom stood over him; blood flowing freely from his torn neck. He bent down and grabbed Deano by his head with both hands, lifted his face to his own so that they were eye to eye.

"You don't deserve to live," Tom sneered, then he head butted him once, twice, three times with superhuman strength. Deano was dead and Tom had collapsed, holding his neck in agony.

Ed rushed to his friend's aid, removing his jacket to place it over Tom's injured neck.

"It hurts Ed, it really hurts. We were going to leave weren't we? We were getting supplies so we can get away from Ged and never look back. You'll have to go on your own now, I can't come with you once I'm a bad man," Tom cried.

"You are still coming with me my friend don't you worry about that. I'm not going to let anything bad happen to you. All we need to do is clean out your wound, dress it properly then you'll feel a lot better, you'll see," Ed reassured.

"Do you know what made me feel better? Hurting Johno and Deano. I've never felt anger like it before and attacking those two dummies made me feel more alive than I have my whole life. It's like the pain in my neck is making me weak but when I'm angry, I feel strong and ALIVE! But what's more Ed, I enjoyed making them suffer. Because they deserved it, they deserved to die and I enjoyed killing them. Really enjoyed killing them! What's happening to me Ed? I never used to be like this?" Tom asked, tears welling as blood continued to pour from his neck, seeping through Ed's jacket.

Ed pulled his friend into his arms and held him in an embrace. He loved Tom and it hurt deeply to see him in so much pain; knowing that it was only a matter of time before the infection took him.

"It burns Ed, I feel heat from my neck spreading across my chest and it's making me angry again. It's the bad man isn't it? He's taking over; he's going to get me!" Tom wept.

Ed helped the big man to his feet and walked him away from the station, stopping at the taxi with the zombie driver secured inside.

"Look at him Tom. That's what a bad man looks like. You look nothing like him do you?" Ed said solemnly.

Whilst Tom looked at the zombie in the taxi, Ed lifted his crowbar and drilled it hard into the back of his friend's head, killing him instantly.

The last thing that Tom saw whilst looking at the bad man through the car window, was his own reflection as the dark rain clouds parted momentarily and a ray of light hit the glass, replacing the taxi driver's face with his own.

Journal Entry 20

"So that's your plan?" I asked, completely flabbergasted at the ridiculousness of my brother's scheme.

"It's fool-proof," he replied.

"It's devised by a fool I know that much! You want us to dress up as zombies and slowly crawl through the Pavilions' grounds, climbing over dead shufflers until we reach the building. Then we sit quietly and wait for Ged to make an appearance and when he does, we jump up, scare the shit out of him, rough him up a bit then make a run for it? Brilliant brother, faultless!" came my reply.

"I'm in!" Emily piped up, eagerly.

"Sneaky twat attack, I like it ace, count me in but there is no chance I'm dressing up as a zombie lar. You see this jacket I'm wearing? I bought this from a girl that used to knob Simon Le Bon from Duran Duran. There is no chance I'm getting zombie gunk on these threads kid," Dave stated.

"So your jacket actually belonged to Simon Le Bon?" Nick asked, impressed.

I am surrounded by lunatics, all battling for top spot in the Zombie Apocalypse League of Mental. Butty has been running away with the lead since before the apocalypse began and now his half -baked plan to pretend to be zombies had all but secured him the title!

After we had discovered Jonathon's killer, who we now knew was called Ged (thanks to his gang after we had overheard them whilst hiding amongst zombies we killed and not being intimate with them in anyway), was only a short walk away, Butty, 80s Dave and I had decided to take a closer look. When we got there we found the large grounds of the sports club to be flooded with dead zombies. I mean, they were everywhere. Like a blanket of corpses that covered every blade of grass with the only clearance being the road leading to the building.

Now we had a very important decision to make. What do we do with this discovery? We joined Emily and the others in the living room of the apartment and shared what we had uncovered and that's when Butty told of his master plan. Emily, filled with rage and hate would have agreed to anything as long as it meant confronting Ged. But come on, really? Zombie fancy dress? It's a long shot at best and with 80s Dave agreeing but refusing to get his retro clothes dirty it had failure written all over it.

"I never said the jacket belonged to Simon Le Bon, just that the girl I bought it from nobbled him a few times that's all. She got around a bit in 80s to be fair and if I recall, she also had a pirate's hat belonging to Adam Ant and the red codpiece worn by Cameo in the music video for their hit single 'Word Up'. She was using that as a hanging basket for a gladioli last I heard," Dave said, answering Nick's question.

The room went quiet for moment, stunned into silence by Dave's incredible ability to switch a conversation from what is important to anything to do with the 1980s.

Whilst everyone was picturing Cameo with a house plant poking out of his codpiece, Nick was the first to get his mind back into the present and on the matter at hand.

"What if the girls stayed here and I went with Dave? We could walk right up to the Pavilions and act as a distraction whilst you guys played undead and sneak attacked Ged?" He suggested.

Butty grinned from ear to ear, "It's like you read my mind! Maybe my old friend Trust No-one taught you a thing or two after all."

"Butty, a word in private if I may big brother," I said sternly.

Butty followed me out onto the hallway and we closed the door behind us, leaving Emily, Nick and the girls listening to 80s Dave as he continued to harp on about Duran Duran and how the extreme amount of hairspray consumed by Nick Rhodes over the last thirty years has single handedly destroyed the Ozone layer. And as much as I enjoy listening to Dave's tales, I needed to talk some sense into Butty in private, without the others encouraging him!

"You can't really believe that this plan of yours is a good idea? Pretending to be zombies to get close to Ged and then what? Beat him up a bit then leg it? That's if your plan works at all and let's be honest here, it's a long shot at best. There are better odds on me suddenly developing a love of mayonnaise or Dave removing his sunglasses. The only thing this plan will achieve is getting us all killed. I've only just got Emily back and I'm damned if I'm going to lose her again. Not a chance Butty, there has to be another way?" I argued.

To my surprise and for only the second time in our lives, Butty actually listened to me. The first time that this phenomenon happened was when we were kids and he had become obsessed with a girl named Karen Forde that lived across the road from us. She was older, more mature, mysterious and for my brother, the perfect woman. He would spend hour after hour, sat in his bedroom window, staring at her house, hoping to see her walk past a window or open the front door. It was all innocent at first and quite funny to watch him swooning over someone that wouldn't give him the time of day. But it quickly moved from admiring her from a far to sitting in her drive way on his Chopper, singing Renee and Renato's 'Save Your Love' every morning before school. Then after a few weeks of his love laden warblings, things had escalated again. I came home one day to find him standing in front of his bedroom mirror taking pictures of himself with a Polaroid camera. Not so strange you might think and you're right, it wouldn't have been, if he wasn't wearing her underwear! He had pinched her knickers and bra from her washing line and thought it would be a good idea to snap himself wearing them and send the pictures to her. He thought it would show how much he loved her! Luckily, and for the first time in his life, he saw sense and listening to me, changed his mind at the very last minute. And it's a good job too as am sure Karen being presented with pictures of him bent over in her knickers would have resulted in the men in white coats coming to take him away. It was around that time he became a full blown apocalypse nut, dedicating all of his free time in preparing for the end of the world. He'd never shown much interest in girls after his obsession with Karen, until recently that is.

"Well there is one other way but it will take a bit of organising and we will still need to get Ged out of the Pavilions and set up a trap. He's too secure in there. Nick seems keen to help…"

"No, absolutely not! Everyone we meet ends up dead. Jonathon, Brittain, Steven… the girl with the Hulk fist and cape could be dead for all we know. We're not getting anyone else killed and besides, he's got the girl and baby, to take care of. They need to be safe and as far away from us as possible. Somewhere secure if there is such a place anymore," I said.

"I've been thinking about that little brother. We have been on the move since my house burnt down and I have been trying to think of somewhere we can go when this is all over. We need somewhere similar to my house. Zombie proof and with enough supplies to keep us going for a while. We can't keep roaming the streets moving from house to house. We wouldn't last more than week if we did that. If zombies don't get us than a paranoid and scared survivor will. There is only one place and one person we can turn to," Butty said, retrieving his C.B. radio from his utility belt, "Sky Watcher!"

Sky Watcher, Butty's secret crush and fellow surviving member of A.R.S.E! Given our circumstances it made sense. She had followed my brother's advice and secured her home under his tutorage. We should be safe there, from zombies at least. Crazy bastards like Ged? Well it appears this town is full of them! Other survivors will always be a threat and we will have to learn how to keep a low profile. Correction, 80s Dave and Butty will have to learn how to keep a low profile. Once we had taken care of Runcorn's craziest of bastards that is!

"Whilst the prospect of living with two apocalyptic crazies doesn't exactly fill me with delight it is the best plan we have. If she's up for taking us in that is? When was the last time you talked to her" I asked.

"Early this morning at Brittain's place. I popped upstairs for a shit whilst you were chatting with Dave in the kitchen, so I checked in to see how she was," he replied.

My face gave a mixed expression of confusion and disgust. Did I just hear right? Did he say he contacted the woman he had a crush on to check if she was still alive whilst sat on a porcelain throne with his pants around his ankles pushing out a poo?

"I'm at my most relaxed when I'm having a poo so why not? I find it easier to talk to people when I'm relaxed. You know how much I hate social contact. I find it difficult communicating face to face never mind over the phone and add to that it's Sky Watcher and well... you know how much I like her. Talking whilst shitting gets me through. Plus, when I'm straining I sound a bit like Clint Eastwood and she likes that." he explained.

Which made me think about the thousands of conversations we've had over the years using a telephone. He must have sensed what I was thinking because before I could ask he looked at me and nodded slowly, "every single one," he said.

Imagining Butty taking a dump whilst talking like Dirty Harry aside, I was sold on the idea of sending Nick and the girls away to Sky Watcher's place. If she was half as batty as my brother, and all evidence was suggesting she was, then they would be safe. A lot safer than staying with us anyway and then, when Jonathon was avenged, we would join them and have a place we could start again.

"Do you think she'll take us in? All of us?" I asked.

"Absolutely. Well, me definitely but I'm sure I can convince her to put us up. It might be only temporary till we find a place of our own. I'll try and get hold of her now on but listen, this plan I have to take care of Ged. It will work but it will take some planning and it's something I need to do on my own. It's dangerous and I need to work quickly and without detection. If you, Emily and Dave come too then you'll only slow me down. If Sky Watcher agrees, I'll take Nick and the kids to her then I'll get everything ready for Ged. You, Emily and Dave stay here and keep an eye on the Pavilions, I'll leave you with a C.B. radio so we can keep in touch but whatever you do, do not make a move on the fucker without me. You'll get yourselves killed. If he moves or if anything changes then speak to me first," he said, pushing a C.B. radio into my hands.

"Are you going to share your plan to extract revenge?" I asked.

"I would but you'd think I was crazy," he replied.

Like I needed any help thinking he was crazy!

Devil At Your Door

Tap, tap, tap, tap, tap, tap...

Ged sat behind the desk in the office of the Pavilions, swaying on his chair whilst tapping the blunt end of a pencil into the wooden surface. The desk was littered with broken pencils, all due to his frustration and impatience.

Tap, tap, tap, tap, tap, tap... SNAP

Another pencil gone.

Also on the desk was Joni's scab covered, decaying head. He had placed his cousin directly in front of him, with a glass of straight Scotch resting next to his chin.

Ged rummaged in the desk draw, flinging paper work to the floor till he found what he was looking for.

Tap, tap, tap, tap, tap, tap...

He looked at the clock, it was late afternoon and Ed, Tom, Johnno and Deano had been gone for a lot longer than expected. He had sent his men out to scavenge for supplies, with the instruction of hitting Runcorn railway station as a priority. Ticket machines and cash machines meant that monetary supplies should be plentiful and the station shop would be a good source for looting food and drink. Ged wasn't stupid, he knew that money had no place anymore but he had one eye on the future and if zombies were to be eradicated then it may once again become a trading commodity.

Tap, tap, tap, tap, tap, tap...

He felt Joni's cold blue eyes glaring at him. His eyes were not always blue. When he was alive they were a dark brown but since his death the loss of pigment and draining of blood from his peepers had caused the colour to change to an icy blue. It was unsettling, even for someone like Ged.

"What is it Joni? Haven't you got anything better to do than stare at me questionably all afternoon? You've not even taken as much as a sip of your whisky and whisky my dear cousin, will soon be difficult to come by."

Tap, tap, tap, tap, tap, tap...

Still he felt Joni's eyes upon him.

"Yes I know what time it is, I've been looking at the clock all afternoon. I am fully aware they should be back by now."

Tap, tap, tap, tap, tap, tap... SNAP

Ged clenched a fist around the broken pencil.

"That was my last pencil," he smarted, pushing his chair back before taking to his feet and pacing the office.

"Oh really Joni? You think that? You think they would turn on me when they know what I'm capable of? Well that's why I'm the boss and you are just a rotting head! After what I did to Paul, chopping his head off in front of them, Johno and Deano wouldn't dare. Plus they are too stupid to turn on me and Ed has always been my most loyal employee. Plus he has that big dumb bastard Tom to take care of. He knows they are safer with me than on their own. Well it comes as no surprise that you'd think that, you've always hated Ed. Even if you're right and they have turned on me, they wouldn't make it far. I'd hunt them down then kill them, slowly and very, very painfully. So that in their final moments all they would think of is me and how if they'd only stayed loyal they wouldn't be about to die!"

Ged looked again to the clock on the wall and to the time, slowly ticking away.

"Fine, you win! We'll go and look for them. Now you've put the idea in my head it's going to be impossible for me to relax anyway. But you're coming with me!"

Ged took his sword in one hand and picked up his cousin's head with the other, cradling it under his arm before leaving the office and entered the long hallway, marching to the main entrance of the building.

Along the hallway were several doors leading to function rooms. Ged had made plans for every room within the Pavilions. The first function room was for storing food, water and general living supplies such as medicine and clothes. The second function room was going to be the armoury, filled with anything and everything that could be used as a weapon against the undead and also, other survivors. Upstairs was a third larger function room. It was the size of both the downstairs rooms combined. This was going to be Ged's trophy room, where he would keep mementos of every 'special' kill he made, both undead and human alike. He only wished he'd acquired the Pavilions earlier or had the forward thinking to take a hand, tongue, leg or even head of the old lady he had killed to take her apartment and from the boy he had tied to a lamppost and set zombies upon to teach those fuckers a lesson from a few nights before. At the moment, the only trophy the large function room held, was the head of Paul Hillan but he intended to fill it.

He pushed open the large doors and exited the building. Before him lay the hundreds of undead corpses that covered the surrounding fields and a small smog, hanging low to the ground hovered over the bodies. It was the thing of nightmares but Ged loved it and admired the view like an art lover soaking in the Café Terrace at Night by Vincent Van Gogh.

"Almost finished boss, just this last window to do then we're secure," said Billy from atop a ladder to Ged's right.

"Me too, we should have enough limbs to cover the entire building," Kitty informed.

To Ged's left, Kitty leant against a large axe and with her free hand, wiped the sweat from her tattoo covered brow. In front of her was a huge pile of chopped up zombies.

"I'll have these nailed onto the walls in no time," she said.

"Leave it for now," Ged replied, "You're coming with me. Billy, you stay here and look after the place till we get back. When you're done here I need you inside to take inventory of all our stock. Joni here seems to think the others have done a runner with our loot. If my cousin is right, then not only am I going to find then murder the treacherous bastards, but we'll be needing to do another supply run."

Ged sat astride Billy's motorbike, mounting Joni's head to the handlebar by shoving an attached mirror up his neck hole, then sliding his sword through the belt loop on his jeans. Kitty climbed upon her bike also.

"How do you like my new GPS?" Ged laughed, "Show me the way Joni!"

Both motorbikes left the Pavilions' grounds and turned onto Sandy Road. Ged immediately brought his bike to a halt, signalling for Kitty to do the same.

Dismounting the bike he walked forward, brandishing his sword, signalling for Kitty to join him. Before them was a road full of dead zombies.

Carefully he continued forward with Kitty not far behind, brandishing a large carving knife. A huge grin filled his face. He loved what he was seeing and eyeing the many dead he became filled with adrenaline, imagining the gory battle that had taken place.

"Do you think Johno and Deano did this?" Kitty asked.

Ged looked further up the road. Tyre imprints from Ed's van and Johno and Deano's motorbikes were visible on bodies on the road.

"No, it was someone else," he grinned.

He took a few more steps forward, inspecting the dead and the wounds to their heads. To his right, a little up the road was the old lady's apartment he had taken shelter in the few days previous and he thought again about removing her head or at least one of her hands to keep as a trophy. Now was as good a time as any to revisit his victim so he approached the apartment cautiously, carefully stepping over the slain zombies.

Then he saw her. The old lady he had murdered was loosely wrapped in a sheet on the road below the apartment window. The sheet that covered her had unravelled exposing her face and the knitting needle wound to her forehead. Then he saw the Ford Thunderbird.

"If Johno and Deano didn't do this then who did? Who the hell killed them all?" Kitty asked.

Ged's eyes opened wide and a wild expression took his face. Joining the adrenalin within was hate and anger. He knew exactly who it was that killed all those zombies and he knew why. They were coming for him, for what he did to the kid.

Not if he got to them first.

Journal Entry 21

Emily sat, holding herself tightly, curled up on the couch. A quilt wrapped around her to keep warm. It was, like always, a cool afternoon but my body felt little of the cold. I was too worried about Butty, his secret but no doubt insane plan and the thought of confronting Ged, to feel the chill. The only thing my body felt was worry!

80s Dave sat in the apartment window keeping an eye on the Pavilions and for Butty to return. He had been gone for several hours now and let me tell you, several hours in a zombie apocalypse, sat in a cold apartment with nothing to do but listen to the tinny music pumping from Dave's headphones feels like days!

My mind was wondering. Flipping from worrying about Butty, to how happy I was to have Emily back then to the depressing truth of our reality. What it meant to be alive in a dead world. I had to snap out of it and although I'd been putting it off, the only person that could help shift the storm cloud forming was Dave and his ability to talk shite or reel off endless facts about anything from the 1980s.

"Spill the beans then Dave, what are you listening to that's had you nodding your head and grinning from ear to ear for the past hour?" I asked.

"Only the greatest soundtrack to one of the greatest movies ever made Ace. Two words John, Teen fucking Wolf! Now I'm not talking about that bollocks MTV series for morons that wouldn't know a good TV show if it kicked them in the knackers, but the 1985 classic starring Michael J Fox as Scott Howard, the high school kid struggling to fit in until he discovers he's a werewolf which makes him a hit with the ladies and awesome at basketball. Not only is the film an all-time classic but the soundtrack is a thing of beauty lar. Pure 80s gold and extremely rare. You're talking anything from thirty green queens up on eBay kid, and that's for a CD. What I'm listening too here is the original cassette. It's worth more than your life!" Dave proclaimed.

And he didn't stop there, he continued, seemingly without pause for breath for the next 20 minutes detailing every song on the album and why they are such classics. He even gave Emily and I a full rendition of 'Win In The End' by Mark Safan, complete with a full enactment of the end of the movie where Scott Howard refuses to be the wolf to help his basketball team win the big game and instead they all pull together to defeat their rivals using good old fashioned team work. As bizarre as it was to watch him pretend to be Michael J Fox playing basketball, it did clear my head a little and for the first time since the world went to shit, I saw Emily laugh.

After Dave had finished his Teen Wolf tribute, conversation turned towards the world we once knew and the things we miss. It was less than a week since the outbreak but the world was already a very different place.

"I miss the internet," Emily said, "especially social media and being able to chat and share pictures with my friends. If it was still working all we'd have to do is log on to Facebook to see who was still alive, set up an 'event' then we could all meet up and start to fight back."

She had a point. Social media dominated western culture and how we communicated with each other. Although, if Facebook was still working it wouldn't be long till our timelines would end up filled with zombie selfies and stupid quizzes called 'Which Zombie Are You?' and 'What Is Your Undead Name?" And stupid memes with a picture of a sad zombie and next to it some nostalgic words about the world before the apocalypse. 'Please share if you remember when you could walk the streets without worrying you might get eaten'. I bet people would still post pictures of their food though.

"I'm glad there's no internet. Facebook, Twatter and bollocks like Instagram or Pinterest have done nothing for the world but make people antisocial and dumb. People spending their evening tending to their virtual farm? Give me a fucking break kid. They should be listening to music, reading a book or educating themselves by watching awesome 80s movies like Summer School, Iron Eagle, Caddyshack, Revenge of the Nerds, Animal House or Police Academy 3! Google is the worst. People don't have to remember or even learn anything anymore, they just type what they want to know into Google and it tells them the answer. I'm glad all that shit is gone because we're back to the good old days like when you couldn't recall the name of the singer from Visage with all the weird make up. Sometimes you'd have to wait days or even weeks for your brain to remember. There was no Google to turn to then. You had to wait till your mind wanted you to know and when it did the answer would always pop in there when you least expected it. You would be on the bus, in an exam, in a meeting or at a funeral surrounded by grieving people when suddenly you'd blurt out STEVE STRANGE and everyone would look at you like you were a knob head! Great days Ace, great days." Dave smiled, lighting a cigarette, "So what do you miss kid?"

"Lazy days at home with Emily," I replied, "visiting Butty for a few drinks at the weekend, listening to his ridiculous conspiracy theories and end of the world scenarios, safe in the belief that none of them would actually happen. Just the simple things really. I'll tell you what I don't miss, working at the mayonnaise factory. You know I've seen a lot and done a lot of disgusting things these last few days but thinking about mayonnaise makes me want to gag just as much now as it ever has. In fact, that's the best thing about the zombie apocalypse, no more mayonnaise!"

The three of us laughed and forgot ourselves for a moment as conversation went back and forth discussing what we did and didn't miss. Emily missed hockey and Dave didn't miss modern music. I didn't miss housework and Dave did miss, as he put it "Taking the piss out of door to door religious pests, trying to convert me to whoever their 'God of the Month' was."

"What I'd do ace," he said, "I'd open the door to them really enthusiastically then invite them in for a brew and I'd tell them that I will sign up to whatever David Icke-esq beliefs they were trying to brainwash me with, just as long as they could rap every line from Rapper's Delight by the Sugarhill Gang. Many tried but not one of the pesky faith peddlers could manage it."

Breaking our conversation was the rumbling of motorbikes approaching. All three of us dove to the floor and Dave peered out of the window discreetly.

"Cunt alert, it's Ged, it's fucking Ged! He's got a woman with him with tattoos covering her bald head. She looks like a fucking marble! And what the hell is that on his bike? Sick lar! He's got a human head stuck to his handle bars!"

I gripped Emily by her arm and shook my head, instructing her not to make a move. I could see the hatred swelling within her.

"Remember what your uncle said. We stay hidden till he gets back," I said.

Where the hell was Butty?

Mission Improbable

"Thanks Sky Watcher, I really appreciate it good buddy," Butty smiled, one hand on the wheel and the other on his C.B. radio.

"Don't mention it Lone Wolf," Sky watcher replied, "the girls are great and Nick is already making himself useful. He's out back chopping up dead zombies right now. You can never have too many limbs nailed to your house, you told me that! I'll see you and your family later, Sky Watcher out."

Butty's heart was still pounding since their first face to face meeting. Both he and Sky Watcher had been flirting over the airwaves for a long time and now he had seen her, he knew she was the one for him. Nothing could have prepared him for how perfect she was.

A vision of apocalyptic beauty greeted him when she yanked open her boarded up window and climbed down that rope ladder. Head to toe in camouflage, stab proof vest and copies of Playgirl, Hunks and Studs Monthly strapped to her arms, Sky Watcher was an angel and Butty was in heaven. On her head she wore a hard hat with A.R.S.E. written on the front. It was love at first sight.

Any doubts he may have had disappeared when he first saw her and to his delight, she too had taken a shine to him. He now had someone other than his brother and niece to live for. Someone he had a chance to build a life with which made the execution of his plan all the more important.

He drove into Runcorn town centre and parked in the bus station. The first step in his plan was to locate a large vehicle, like a truck, wagon or an abandoned bus, the latter he was hoping to find but there was nothing. Just a plentiful display of dead zombies and an up turned portable toilet.

He left his vehicle and inspected the bus station on foot. It soon became evident that there had been a battle and approaching the broken toilet he spied three dead bodies which had been alive when they were killed. All three them, which included one in a polka dot dress, had trauma wounds to their heads and surrounding them, motorbike tracks. The only people he had encountered with motorbikes were Ged's men and having witnessed first-hand what they were capable of, he was in no doubt that they were responsible.

He heard a vehicle and took cover, hiding behind the broken toilet, covertly watching as the blue transit van that belonged to Ged pulled up into the bus station and a man he did not know stepped out, walking towards his location.

Ed needed more than the supplies he took from the train station if he was to leave town. He needed weapons and something more substantial to eat. Unlike Tom, he couldn't survive on sugary confectionary alone. He had decided to make a short stop in Runcorn town centre. There was hardware shops and supermarkets close by and his plan was to quickly gather as much weaponry and food as he could then leave, before Ged, Billy and Kitty came looking.

Pulling up in the bus station he looked at the zombie massacre before him and hoped that whoever did this had long left the area.

Leaving the van he cautiously approached the dead zombies, a large knife hidden behind his back should he need it. Then he saw the three dead men and the motorbike tracks.

"Bastards!" Ed exclaimed.

'CHHH!' Butty's C.B. radio crackled to life.

"Dave to Crazy Ace, come in Crazy Ace, do you copy, over?" Came Dave's voice over the C.B. radio.

He scrambled to turn off his radio but Ed had already heard.

"Who's there? Come out, show yourself!" Ed demanded, gripping a concealed knife behind his back.

With little point in staying hidden Butty stepped out from behind the portable toilet and Ed's jaw dropped.

"I know you! You and your friend, you stole our supplies and killed Joni. You killed Ged's cousin!" Ed pronounced.

"Joni? You mean that scabby headed dip shit that fell out of your van and cracked his head open? We never touched him mate, the numpty killed himself. But you, there's plenty of blood on your hands," Butty snarled, readying his crowbar for action.

"I'm not with Ged and the others, not anymore anyway, not after everything they've done." Ed replied.

"What do you mean?" Butty quizzed. "I saw you with them earlier, heading out for supplies."

"I did but Tom and me, we… Well I left. I'm never going back," he affirmed.

Ed explained what had happened at the train station and how he had been waiting for an opportunity for him and Tom to escape. To get as far away from Ged as possible.

"He's dangerous, ruthless and psychotic. Ged doesn't care who he hurts just as long as he gets what he wants and now he's reconnected with the rest of his gang, well what's left of them. There's something about the end of the world that brings the lunatic out in people," Ed said.

Butty lowered his crowbar. It was clear that Ed was not a threat. Then the bus station echoed with the sound of groaning and a small scattering of zombies approached, closing in on the two men.

Ed pulled out his knife and Butty raised his crowbar.

"I hope you know how to use that? Ed asked nervously.

Butty swooped the crowbar low at the nearest zombie, taking out its legs leaving it squirming on the ground. Then, using his heavy boots he jumped into the air and stomped on its head, crushing its skull. Using the zombie's torso like a doormat he wiped his boots clean.

"You could have just hit the head, there was no need to jump on it like that!" Ed squirmed.

"It's fun to be creative, keeps me on my toes," Butty smiled in reply.

With two shufflers closing in behind him, Ed turned and stabbed the knife into their heads whilst Butty continued his onslaught, taking out zombie after zombie. Soon the small horde was cleared and the two men stood victorious.

"You said you will never go back to Ged. Well I plan to take him out for good but I could do with your help. I need your van and these three dead men," Butty said, pointing his bloodied crowbar at their corpses, "What do you say? Are you in?"

Journal Entry 22

"Come on out fuckers! I know you're in there and I know why you're here. This is what you want right? To face me? To make me pay for killing the kid? Well I'm waiting..." Ged yelled from below our window.

Emily was furious, her skin turning a blotchy red with rage.

"Let me go Dad," she fumed, "I need this, I need to face him!"

I refused to let her go, gripping her arm tight.

"We can take him Ace, there's three of us and only him and the woman with a tattooed head that looks like a gob stopper. Let's get down there and sort the prick out once and for all. We could end this now," Dave raged, twizzling the Battle Paddle in his hands.

Take him out? Who did he think we were, The Krays? Between us we had a hammer, a crowbar and an oversized badly burnt spoon. Not exactly a formidable arsenal against a serial killer with a Samurai sword!

We had found ourselves in an impossible situation. If we left the apartment and confronted Ged outside, we may win the numbers game but we would be facing two fearless psychopaths, that wouldn't think twice about killing us. Now killing zombies is one thing but people, no matter how evil they are, is something else entirely.

Our other option was to stay put and wait for Ged to come to us which would give us a tactical advantage. Both options had the same outcome. Bloodshed.

"Come out, face me! You wanted this, come and get what you came for!" Ged sneered from the road below.

Emily was almost growling she was so angry. He was taunting us; this is exactly what he wanted.

"Everyone just calm down, let's think about this for a minute and not do anything rash. We should let him sweat for now. If he decides he's had enough and comes for us then we'll defend ourselves. Otherwise we stay put and wait for Butty to get back. Remember, he told us not to do anything till he returns," I said, trying to stay calm.

"OK Ace, your call but remember, your brother also straps wank mags to his arms and drinks his own piss. It's true, I saw him filling up his drinks canister this morning. He had his lash dipped right in there. I asked him why he was drinking his own slash and he said he's been drinking it for years! He said it's so he could get used to the taste before water supplies run out. He said he likes it! Apparently, the amount of spam he eats makes his waz taste like bacon. So what I'm saying is, maybe Butty's advice isn't always the best advice." Dave suggested.

"What if Uncle Butty doesn't come back Dad?" Emily asked solemnly, "We need a plan B."

A plan B? We didn't know what Plan A was yet!

I peeped out of the window. Ged was pacing back and forth, directly below the apartment window on the road outside. As he walked he was stabbing and slicing his sword into dead zombies, hacking at them in anger.

Come on Butty, where the hell are you?

Ged was quickly losing patience, not that he possessed that much to begin with. He glanced up to the window and saw a man peeping back at him. He wanted them dead and wished they had all perished in the house fire he caused a few nights earlier or that he'd set zombies on them like he did the kid he had taken from the basement. But his thought of what might have been was fleeting for now he had a chance to kill them again and in a way much more suited to his murderous desires. Up close and personal. One on one and eye to eye. His biggest thrill of all was to watch the life leave his victims. Like when he stabbed the old lady in her forehead. For Ged it felt like her life ending breathed new life into his. A rush, a high, an injection of adrenalin. It was a feeling he loved more than anything and he was desperate to feel it again. If only he could think of a way to lure them outside.

"What if you two stay here and I go down and challenge him to a duel? His sword against my Battle Paddle. I know which I'd place money on Ace. Or even better, I could challenge him to a sing off! The loser has to fuck off and never come back. To win you have to perform a word perfect rendition of Virginia Plain by Roxy Music. Nobody knows what Bryan Ferry was singing in that one lar, even the man himself couldn't tell you what he was blabbering on about. Except for me that is! I bought the copy of Smash Hits Magazine that had the words in. I'd wipe the floor with the prick!" Dave said excitedly.

As ridiculous as Dave's suggestions were, he was deadly serious and I was honoured that once again, my retro piss taking 80s obsessed friend was willing to put it all on the line for Emily and I. I don't know where I'd be without him. Dead probably!

But I couldn't let him do it. I was adamant we were sticking together, to wait for Butty to return. But with time moving on and no sign of my brother a little doubt was starting to creep in. What if Emily was right? What if he never returns? It's a dangerous world out there, anything could have happened to him. Then I remembered he'd left us with a C.B. radio so we could contact him in case of an emergency and being the fucking genius that I am, I had completely forgotten about it and left it in the hallway.

Crawling across the floor so as not to be seen from the window, I retrieved the C.B. radio and returned to the others. Although I had seen Butty use one on many an occasion, I was a novice. Apart from turning it on and off I didn't have a clue.

"Butty said that if we get into trouble we should contact him through this thing. Anyone know how to use it? Emily? Your uncle has been getting you ready for the end of the world for years; did he never show you how to work one of these?" I asked hopefully.

"I've seen one before but he would never let me use one unless I became a member of A.R.S.E. but as I don't believe in a race of reptile alien's that have hollowed out the moon and are using it to prepare for an invasion, I don't qualify. What operating system does it use?" she replied looking at it with confusion.

"Operating system? Retro 4.0 lar! Honestly, you kids today. There was a world before smartphones you know. Back in the day, kids used to walk around with one of these bad boys glued to the hands like you lot do today with your phones. Only instead of blasting out shit music, snapchatting, facetiming or whatever it is you do, kids used to use a C.B. radio to chat to each other. Well, mostly try to pick up girls by chatting to them in secret code, pretending to be truckers whilst walking the streets trying to figure out where they lived. Great days! Give it here lar, I'll try and contact him. I've watched Smokey and Bandit more times than I'd like to admit to so I should be able to work it," Dave said, taking the radio.

"Dave to Crazy Ace, come in Crazy Ace, do you copy, over?" Dave spoke into the C.B. radio.

No response.

"Butty, this is Dave lar. If you can hear my majestic voice please respond?" he continued.

Still nothing.

"Come ed' Daddy O', open a fucking channel kid!" Dave groaned.

This wasn't looking good. Why the hell wasn't he responding? Had the unthinkable happened and Butty had found himself in trouble he couldn't get out of? Maybe he was trapped somewhere and couldn't raise the alarm by using the radio. Or maybe it was a lot worse and his solo mission had ended with him paying the ultimate price.

I had never before this moment contemplated that anything bad could happen to Butty. He is made for an apocalyptic world. If anyone was built to survive a zombie apocalypse it was him.

"It doesn't mean anything kid. He could be driving or more than likely he's having fun bashing zombie heads. Hey, maybe when he dropped Nick and the girls off at Sky Watchers, his dreams came true and they hit it off. They could be in the sack now, busy trying to repopulate the human race!" Dave suggested.

I am not sure what was worse. The thought of my brother being dead or a world populated with his spawn. Imagine, a world full of mini Butty's, eating nothing but spam and drinking their own piss!

Ged had waited long enough. Time was up for the people in the apartment. He desperately needed a way to force them outside. Rushing the apartment to confront them was not a desired option and would put him and Kitty at a distinct disadvantage. No, he wanted them out in the open.

Pacing back and force his attention was once again taken with the old lady wrapped in a sheet.

"You want a cigar boss? Kitty offered.

He turned to see Kitty, striking a match on the back of her head then lighting a huge cigar.

This gave him an idea.

Time was moving slowly and it felt like Ged had been at our window for eternity. Every attempt to contact Butty had failed. We were on

165

our own and facing up to the loony tune outside was looking inevitable.

Dave and Emily had gone to search the apartment to see if there was anything else we could add to our awesome armoury whilst I continued in vein to contact Butty. Dave was the first to return.

"You won't believe how many tins of rice pudding I found in that kitchen lar. I think the old dear that lived here ate nothing else. She can't have had a solid shit for years! There wasn't much we could use as weapons though kid, only this bread knife," Dave said, swooshing the knife, "Suppose we could throw the tins of rice pudding out the window like missiles. Hey, I'll tell you what I did find, check this out Ace."

From behind his back, Dave presented me with an extra- large jar of mayonnaise.

"Look at the label kid, it was made at the factory which means I probably made it and you would have tested it. How cool is that? Maybe you can use it to force feed mayo to Ged so the bastard chokes to death? Death by mayo!" He smiled, throwing me the large jar of the devil's condiment.

Emily returned from the bedroom carrying a walking stick.

"This is all I could find," she said angrily. The only other things in there are packs of incontinence pads."

Incontinence pads. I could have done with wearing those several times over the last few days! I wish I had been wearing one when Ged turned up!

Using knitting cotton, Emily tied the bread knife to the base of the walking stick and created a make shift spear, adding another weapon to our intimidating arsenal. Plus, we also had rice pudding missiles to launch if need be.

"Now what do we do, just wait? Can I at least spark a tab? I'm dying for a smoke." Dave asked.

At that moment the apartment window smashed and we all dove for cover. I could smell what shattered the window before I could see it.

"Fucking sick!" Dave grimaced.

Burning into the shag pile carpet was the decapitated head of an old lady, wrapped in a flaming bed sheet.

"This is her apartment. I found her dead in that chair so I wrapped her up and dropped her out of the window," Emily said.

Dave and I looked at her in shock.

"What?" She was stinking up the place!" Came the defensive reply.

She is definitely her uncle's niece!

Next through the broken window came a flaming hand, followed by a blazing leg then a smouldering foot. I looked to the street below to find Ged stood over the hacked remains of the old lady, proudly displaying his bloodied sword in one hand and one of her arms wrapped in a fiery rag in his other.

"If you won't come out willingly, I'm going to smoke you out!" Ged yelled, launching the arm towards the window.

The old lady's arm came through the window and landed on her knitting supplies. The wool and cotton quickly ignited, bursting into flames. I removed my jacket to smother the fire whilst Dave stomped out the pockets of flames caused by the burning appendages. In the chaos neither of us noticed that Emily had made a dash for the exit.

I ran to the window. Emily was outside, squaring off against Ged and the tattoo headed women. She was brandishing the walking stick / bread knife spear and Ged was howling with laughter.

"That's how you think you're going to kill me? With that? GET HER KITTY!" he screamed.

Kitty made a dash towards Emily but my daughter, reacted quickly and threw the make shift spear like a javelin towards the woman, spiking her through the forehead with the bread knife. She was dead and Emily went into shock. Like a trembling statue she was frozen to the spot.

Ged watched the weapon he mocked glide past his face and penetrate the women's head. She died instantly but stayed on her feet for a few moments. A small slither of blood trickled from the wound, running down her nose and into her open mouth. Then she fell backwards, hitting the road heavily.

Ged's hysterical laughter returned as he pointed at the dead woman. Then he stopped suddenly and his face changed to what I can only describe as pure evil. He pointed his sword at my daughter who was still static.

"Now I kill you!" he sneered.

He ran towards Emily, his sword raised high ready to strike.

"Ace!" Dave yelled, throwing me the large jar of mayonnaise.

Giving it everything I had I hurled the mayonnaise out of the window and with luck on my side, the jar connected with Ged, whacking the bastard on the side of the head.

The impact caused him to drop his sword and fall to his knees dazed. Dave and I ran downstairs and out of the apartment, pulling Emily from the road, away from Ged. Then we saw the blue transit van drive up behind him and I again wished I was wearing one of the old women's incontinence pads! Just when I thought we were going to catch a break, back up arrived.

Ged gave the van a groggy smile and staggered to his feet, retrieving his sword. Driving the van was a man I had never seen before, not properly anyway. I can only assume it was the same man that was driving the night he killed Jonathon.

"Ed! I knew you wouldn't leave me! I told you Joni," He slurred woozily, pointing at the manky head stuck to the handlebars of the motorbike, "I told you he'd be back!"

He turned from the van and walked slowly back towards us, shaking his head in an attempt to clear his vision. The way he was moving, I'd say the mayo missile had given him a concussion. He was all over the place. But despite his injury he continued forward and his face changed again. Back to pure evil!

"AND NOW YOU ARE ALL GOING TO FUCKING DIE!" he screamed manically.

The man driving the blue van started the engine and began reversing.

"Hey, where the fuck are you going?" Ged yelled.

The van continued to reserve then pulled a U-turn so that the rear doors were facing Ged. It then reversed again, moving closer to the sword wielding lunatic.

The driver exited the van then walked towards its rear doors.

"Go to hell!" he shouted.

He opened the rear doors and rushed back to the driver's seat. I couldn't believe what I was seeing and neither for that matter could Ged judging by his reaction. Out of the back of the van, squawked and waddled dozens of frenzied ducks and geese. The noise was horrifying as they frantically moved forward towards Ged.

Quickly they were upon him and he swung his sword, stabbing and slicing at any that came close enough but the bastard didn't stand a chance. He was completely surrounded and still groggy from my mayo missile. If it wasn't so disgusting to watch I would have had a grin like a Cheshire cat! The maniac birds pecked, nipped and pulled at his skin, pouncing on him one by one till he was forced to the ground.

Ged shrieked in agony, his cries echoing up and down Sandy Lane. Behind us we heard another vehicle approaching. It was Butty!

"Get in!" he shouted, poking his camouflaged head out of the driver's window of his Land Rover.

With blood soaked ducks and geese devouring the dying Ged, Butty drove us away.

"Where have you been, we thought you were dead? Why didn't you contact us?" I roared at my brother.

"Dead? Please little brother. It takes more than a zombie apocalypse to kill me! How do you like my plan? Beautiful isn't it? I only wish we could stick around to watch them eat the little bell end but those birds are crazy. It took everything we had to herd them onto the van. Snappy little shits," he replied.

"This was all you Ace? Class lar, if not completely insane. Hats off Butty lad!" Dave applauded, tipping his baseball cap in approval.

"I didn't tell you did I? For some reason, and for the life of me I can't figure out why, ducks and geese have become zombies too. No other animals seem to be affected, just ducks and geese. I considered herding normal zombies to take him out but I thought this had more of a 'WOW' factor.

As he drove away, Butty told us about his plan. About taking Nick and the girls to Sky Watcher's, finding Ed and how the two of them worked together to gather the zombie birds.

"I still can't believe you thought I was dead. Shame on you little brother. What's up with our Emily? She's as white as a sheet."

Emily was sat beside Dave in the back of the car, still in a state of shock and despair. I whispered to Butty about what happened and he slammed on the brakes suddenly, causing us all to jolt forward quickly.

"Shit a brick lar, me head phones nearly flew of me head then!"

171

Butty turned to Emily and looked at her hardheartedly.

"Emily, don't dwell on what you did. She would have killed you, your dad and Dave if she could have. You made sure that didn't happen. You saved, including your own, three lives today. Arseholes like her and Ged, they have the devil in them. They are worse than the undead. Zombies can't reason and they can't make a decision. It's not their choice to eat people. It's just what they do. Ged and that woman, they made a choice to be who they are. The world is better because of what you did today. I would have done exactly the same in your position. Now chin up chuck and remember, what you did was for Jonathon."

Emily didn't speak but she did look at her uncle and gave him a thin smile. At least that was something and I'd have taken anything over nothing at that moment.

"You're damn right it was Ace! Here's to skinny jeans!" Dave toasted, raising a cigarette in Jonathon's name.

"We best get moving. It's getting dark and Sky Watcher is expecting us," Butty said, putting the car into gear and speeding away.

When we reached Sky Watcher's house I was filled with Deja vu. The house, a large semi-detached property, and the neighbourhood, a small cul-de-sac located close to fields and a large water tower did not look familiar. We were in an area of Runcorn I knew little about but the armour to the house and zombie traps set up around it reeked of my brother's work.

Large stakes has been dug into the ground around the house, placed on an angle so that approaching zombies would impale themselves. Although no zombies were speared, many of the stakes were blood stained and on the floor around them lay spilled zombie guts. It didn't take a genius to figure out where all the zombies had gone. All you had to do was look at the house. I could hardy make out the brick work because there was so many zombie limbs nailed to it. Sky Watcher had followed my brother's advice then taken things to another level. The Runcorn League of Mental now had a new entrant and she was storming to the top of the charts!

Leaving the car we approached the front of the property, standing outside the front door. The smell of decomposing flesh was overpowering. A mixture of sickly sweat and rotting eggs! Emily placed her hands over her mouth and nose and as expected, I retched, hard. Puking up what remained in my stomach.

A boarded up window creaked open and a female face, heavily camouflaged peered out.

"He can only come in if he promises not to throw up. If I see one spittle of puke he can get fucked and live in the shed!" she said.

Great, a female version of my brother, exactly what I needed!

A rope ladder dropped for us to climb and Butty looked to me and smiled.

"Home sweet home," he grinned.

This, survivors, brings my journal up to date. As I sit here, in a room surrounded by tins of spam, I can hear my brother through the wall, telling Sky Watcher how he single handily saved our lives with his quick thinking to down the villainous Ged and his gang. I'll let him have his moment and judging by the cooing I can hear from the next room, Sky Watcher is impressed. I think I'll leave it for a few days and let him have his time in the sun. Then I'll tell her that he hasn't changed his underwear for months and he drinks his own piss.

Emily is in the kitchen with Nick and Sophie whilst baby Gaby sleeps. They are cooking dinner which is, you guessed it, spam. Only they are trying to ponce it up by calling it 'spam cooked three ways'. Boiled, grilled and raw.

It's good to see Emily doing something and getting involved. I know she's suffering but keeping busy will do her the world of good. Butty's talk had helped a great deal. It's difficult being a father and not knowing what to do when your child is upset. But when it comes to apocalyptic matters, Butty is more qualified than me. All I could do is be there for her. But I fear the events of the last few days have changed her forever.

80s Dave? Well he's sat opposite me, smoking a tab, still wearing shades and bobbing his head to music through his retro headphones. I'd ask him what he's listening to but if I did I'd never get this journal entry finished.

I'm sat here writing this journal whilst reflecting on the events of the past week. The people we've met, friends we've made and the lives that have been lost. Barry at the newsagents, my stinky boss Simon, reversing the Thunderbird and knocking the undead head off Emily's best friend Jane. Jonathon, Ed, Steven, Brittain, Rod of the Dead, the pompous headmaster Mr Kelly and Emily's depressed class mate Louise, the girl with the cape and Hulk fist with an insatiable appetite for killing zombies, Nick, Sophie and baby Gaby, Brockers who's love of drawing penises resulted in Dave drawing one on his undead forehead, then of course there is Ged and his gang of murderous bastards.

After everything we've gone through I could quite happily sit here and never go outside again but Butty, to no surprise to anyone, has other ideas.

Sky Watchers house is in a small cul-de-sac of other, semi-detached houses. Twelve in total and hers is the only one that's occupied. The other residents had either fled their homes, died or become zombies and ended up nailed to this house. Butty's plan is to secure the whole cul-de-sac by building walls, a gated entrance and look out towers. He wants to call it Apocalypse Street! I have to admit it does have a nice sound to it. The only person that didn't like the name is 80s Dave. He said we should call it Electric Avenue.

Well, I'm beat and there is a sleeping bag and a pillow here with my name on. Hopefully, sleep will come a lot easier tonight, not just for me but for all of us. Butty wants us up bright and early to start on Apocalypse Street. He wants us to search and secure each house, making sure every last one is clear of zombies and then he wants us to start work on fortifying the street. This will no doubt involve an eventful road trip to source building materials. But at least tomorrow marks a new chapter in the post-apocalyptic lives of the Diant family. A new day and a new start. A chance for us to rebuild.

Goodnight all.

Alright Daddy O's, 80s Dave here. Whilst John is fast asleep, dribbling on his pillow, I've had off with his journal to give it a quick shufty. For days I've been asking him to let me have a read but he keeps saying no. Like his private memoirs might one day be of historical significance! Who the fuck does he think he is? Anne Frank? Anyway, I've given it the once over and I just want to clear a few things up as I don't think he's put me across in the best light.

Firstly, my name isn't 80's Dave. I fucking hate the 80s. I detest everything about that decade. The stupid music, terrible fashion, appalling movies and yuppie self-indulgent culture make the 1980s the worst decade in living memory.

My real name is 70s Steve, and I fucking love the 1970s!

Flared trousers, platform shoes, long hair with ridiculous sideburns and pornstar moustaches. And the music lar, you can't beat disco or glam rock! Slade, Mark Bolan, Led Zeppelin and for a dose of the psychedelic, Hawkwind!

Ford Thunderbird? I wouldn't be seen dead driving that heap of junk. It's a Rover SD 1 all the way kidda. British engineering at its best. So what if one side was longer than the other, they don't make them like that anymore!

Double Denim and a 'Choose Life' t-shirt? I don't think so lar. I wouldn't be seen alive never mind dead in those threads! Give me a nylon tracksuit any day. So what if you risked your life every time someone lit a match or you walked past a candle. Or that your clothes were so full of static that stray cats used to stick to you when you walked down the street. It's better than looking like Andrew fucking Ridgeley.

Only joking aces and acettes. Of course my name is 80s Dave! There's no-one else like me lar. 70s Steve my arse. As if I'd like anything from a decade where nearly everyone from British TV turned out to be a sex offender!

I had you going though didn't I? I do have a few gripes about how John has portrayed me though.

For instance, he makes out that I smoke a lot but this isn't true. I don't smoke A LOT, I smoke, ALL THE FUCKING TIME KIDDOS! If you ever see me without a tab hanging out of my mouth then one of two things has happened. Either I'm sick or aliens have kidnapped me and I have been turned into an evil 80s Dave cyborg, hell bent on destroying the earth using my awesome wit and excellent Battle Paddle skills!

Also, he keeps describing the music from my headphones as 'tinny', when it's not; it's fucking BOSS! But what would he know eh? The last album he bought was The Bodyguard soundtrack. He wouldn't know a good track even if it walked right up to him and said, "Hi, I'm Rip It Up by Orange Juice, play the shit out of me right now!"

And another thing. He says I rant about the 80s. I don't rant, I educate. I am an ambassador for the most awesome decade of all time and it is my duty to spread the electric, synthtastic, decadent, shoulder pad wearing, hairspray filled, legwarmer covered, double denim gospel kiddos!

Apart from that, every word is true, even down to John's over the top hatred of mayonnaise!

Anyway kiddas, kiddos, kids, lars, aces and acettes, I'm off for a smoke, a shit and a kip, in that order. Until we meet again!

177

Laters lar!

My Diary

By Butty, age 39 ½

Friday 15th February

Bingo!

A meteor has crashed in Russia, landing in a lake right next to a nuclear power plant. The region is known to be the most polluted place on earth.

There is a strong buzz over the A.R.S.E. network about this, prompting me to yet again start an apocalypse diary but unlike my Robot Uprising journal, Alien Lizard People Invasion Memoirs or my Diary Of A Soon To be Mutated Cyborg Government Experiment, I'm not committing myself to an end of days scenario just yet, in case it turns out to be a false lead. I wouldn't want to look foolish.

I have a very good feeling about this one though. At last this could be the one!

Saturday 16th February

The internet has gone nuts over this meteor. There are videos filling up YouTube showing it flying through the sky heading towards the earth then you hear a massive crash and there is a blinding flash of light. Believe Nothing thinks it never landed in the lake and that it actually hit the nuclear power plant causing it to explode. He thinks it's all a cover up and the Russians are trying to keep a lid on things. Sky Watcher, Trust No One and Truth is Out There agree.

I like talking to Sky Watcher, she makes my palms sweaty.

Sunday 17th February

There is nothing coming out of Russia. No news reports, no nothing. It's like the whole country is on lock down. I can't find any official confirmation of this, there seems to be a media blackout. Even Google is throwing back zero results when I type anything to do with the meteor crash. It's as if it never happened. But we know that something sinister is going on and the only evidence of this is one video, which as quickly as it was uploaded, was taken down again. Fortunately for A.R.S.E. Trust No One managed to rip a copy. The video is of a street in the Russian town of Yekaterinburg. Birds have fallen from the sky and lay dead in the road. People are running for their lives, screaming for help. A police officer is appealing for calm when a women staggers towards him and bites into his face, ripping his cheek clean off! Honestly you should see it. She chows down on that cheek like she hasn't eaten for a month. Then the video ends.

I only had to see that video once to know what this is. ZOMBIES! The day I have been waiting for my whole life is here. If my research is correct then this thing will go global within in a week, maybe even a couple of days. It all depends how the infection spreads but one thing is for sure, we all need to be prepared.

I told the rest of A.R.S.E. what I believe this to be and Sky Watcher and Truth Is Out There agree. Trust No One, the stubborn old git, is having none of it and believes it's an alien virus designed to make us turn on each other. I plan on working on him tonight to make him see sense.

After chatting to my A.R.S.E. mates I made a list of alterations that I need to make to my house. They are:

1.   Board up all windows,

2.   Lock and secure front and back exits to the house,

3.   Build a rope ladder,

4.   Move a large selection of food and weapon supplies from the cellar to the spare bedroom,

5.   Make the back garden fences higher and more secure,

6.   Set zombie traps in the front garden (may need a trip to B&Q for wooden stakes).

I think I might also remove the stairs as a precaution and live on the first floor, only going to the ground level when need be. If this is as bad as I expect it to be then there's a chance zombies could force their way into the house and I'll be safer living off the ground.

Luckily, my years of anticipating the end of the word mean I have two large generators in the cellar so when the power goes out, I'll be fine for a while and I've been hoarding Spam for years so food won't be a problem. I'll get to work straight away, right after I've called my brother to warn him and my niece.

Monday 18th February

I spent most of the night talking to Trust No One over the airwaves and searching the internet for any information regarding the outbreak. Luckily, I managed to talk him around and he's now willing to accept that this is zombies. Although he is adamant that the outbreak has been caused by an alien virus that was inside the asteroid that crashed and aliens are turning people into zombies then when the human race is on its knees, they will appear and take us all out, claiming the planet for their own. It's possible I suppose, I'm just glad he's listening and preparing to defend himself.

Still nothing coming out of Russia but there are hundreds of videos on YouTube showing birds dropping from the sky posted from Georgia, the Ukraine, Romania and Croatia amongst others. Whilst there's still a media blackout in Russia, governments are trying to say there is a new virus affecting birds but it is not a threat to humans. Utter bollocks!

I've no idea what John is playing at. His phone is off and I even went out of my way to pop round his gaff this afternoon whilst I was out shopping for more supplies but there was no answer. He's either pulling in extra shifts at the mayo factory or he's ignoring me on purpose.

I went shopping today for extra supplies. You can never have too much spam and it may have taken me most of the day but I have bought every tin from every supermarket in Runcorn, Widnes, Northwich, Warrington and Wigan. I bought so much that I didn't have room for any water supplies so I'll have to go out again tomorrow but I'm not too bothered about that. Luckily, I have been drinking my own urine for years in preparation for the end of the world. Now I'm not stupid, I know that man cannot survive by only drinking his own piss. That is why I will need to stock up on water supplies but water can be rationed, and sipping it in small quantities whilst slurping down slash to quench your thirst is the best way to stay hydrated.

Tuesday 19th February

The house is now fully stocked with supplies. I have enough to keep me, John and Emily going for a long time, if my ignorant brother ever answered his phone that is. What the hell is he playing at? We're going to have zombies up our arses any day now and he is nowhere to found. I just hope the years of telling John and Emily that in the event of a zombie apocalypse they should get to my place, will be enough. I can't keep trying to get hold of them, there is too much to do around here.

As well as stocking up on supplies, I have now completed all added security work to the house. The windows are boarded up and I've added extra panels to the garden fencing to make them higher. To make the rope ladder, I removed rope from a child's climbing frame in the local park, which was met with some very angry responses, mostly from the children that were using it at the time.

Now I'm not normally so cold hearted that I would take things from children but at the end of the day, they'll all be dead in a week and I'll need to get in and out of my house.

Talking of angry responses. Now over the years I have gotten used to my neighbours looking down at me. I am fully aware they all think I'm mad and to be fair that's how I think about them. For a long time I've had to put up with them talking about me behind my back, complaining about how unkempt my garden is and how run down I've let the house become and that I'm ruining the street. But whilst they've been mowing their lawns to an inch of its life, painting their fences, weeding their gardens and generally keeping up with the Jones; I've been preparing for the end of world. We'll soon see who's mad. Paula next door is the worst. Moaning to the council, the environmental health and putting notes through my door saying the state of my house is devaluing hers. If it wasn't for the fact that she sunbathes topless in her garden, I probably would have said something to her by now but as it stands I've kept quiet. Even this morning when she was stood outside calling me a psychopath for boarding up the windows, I didn't say anything. I've got a plan for her though. I intend to decapitate a few zombies and display their heads on spikes outside the house. This is to warn off other survivors that might be looking to ransack or take shelter in my house. Paula's head is going centre stage right outside my front door!

Right, I'm off for some grub and to check in with A.R.S.E. to see if anymore reports are coming in from Europe.

Wednesday 20th February

I have decided to attempt to wean myself off sleep. The idea is to sleep less and less each night and substitute this with 5 minute power naps throughout the day. I have tried this only once before but it didn't go quite as planned. Not that I remember much about it to be honest but the police and newspaper reports said that I ended up in Asda, naked apart from a crocodile glove puppet covering my penis, and I was smearing myself in Greek yoghurt whilst proclaiming to be the son of Zeus. The reports said I was shouting "My name is Hercules, come take a ride with me upon my mighty steed," whilst pointing to my dick covered sock puppet, swinging it about like a helicopter.

Fortunately I don't remember any of it and as I always say, if you don't remember then it didn't happen. Unfortunately, the judge didn't agree and I got 120 hours community service and banned from shopping in Asda for life. On the plus side, it now means that the rest of A.R.S.E. still have somewhere to get their spam because everywhere else has sold out.

I was in contact with Trust No one and Sky Watcher last night. Sky Watcher has followed my lead by boarding up her house and stocking up on supplies. Trust No One lives in a high rise apartment block so I've told him to come here before the shit hits the fan. He's a stubborn old bastard though. It wouldn't surprise me if he stays put.

Believe Nothing wasn't on air last night, which isn't like him. I hope he's ok.

There is a hell of a lot more buzz on line now. Again, the Russians are keeping quiet but reports of 'rioting' and more bird deaths are coming in from across Europe. It won't be long till it hits the UK.

Thursday 21st February

I finally finished removing the stairs today. To replace them I nailed in two hooks to the floor of the upstairs landing so I can attach the rope ladder. The only time I will be needing to go down there is for repairs or to operate the generators when the power fails and to retrieve supplies from the cellar. I have moved everything else I need upstairs. I used the wood from the stairs to secure both the front and back doors. The only way in and out of the house now, is through the front and back bedroom windows.

The neighbours' curtains are twitching again and Ian from over the road even called the police as he thought I had gone insane and become a serial killer. I know this because he was outside the house last night yelling that the police were coming and he knew what I was up to. Moron. I'm still waiting for the police to turn up but on the plus side, I now have another head to stick on a spike outside my front door. He can keep Paula company.

Got to go as it's almost time for my five minute power nap, then I have to design my zombie survival armour which will mean another trip to the shops. I can't wait for a few weeks when everyone is dead and I can pop out without having to deal with people.

Update –

Hime not slur my plan if weaning meself off sleep is woking. It was goings well tull thi evening when I started to ge a headache in my eyes and vishion has blurry. I th I migh need a coffee to hekp woke me..........

Saturday 23rd February

It's Saturday evening and I've been asleep for nearly two days! TWO FLIPPIN' DAYS! I've got so much to catch up with I best get started but note to self and anyone reading this. Do not try and wean yourself off sleep, it doesn't work. At least I only passed out and didn't get naked, thinking I was Hercules again. The neighbours would have had me sent to the loony bin.

Sunday 24th February

It has been non stop here for two days. I've been trying to catch up after my disastrous attempt to quit sleeping. Back on track now though and just in time too as reports are coming in of pockets of violence happening in London, Birmingham, Southampton, Edinburgh and even as close as Manchester. For once, it has made headline news but as expected it is being reported as rioting and violent protests against the Government and the economic decline of the country. It looks like governments and mainstream media are going to try and keep a lid on this right till the very end.

I've decided to camp out on the roof tonight. I've got a tent up and I have easy access to the house through the sky light in the attic. That way I can keep a look out for any signs of zombies.

My apocalypse armour is now complete. To be honest, I already had everything I needed apart from porno mags but I bought enough yesterday to protect me for a while. It took a lot longer than I had thought, buying grumble magazines. I had to visit every newsagent in town and a lot of them don't put them out on the shelves. They keep them under the counter and make you ask. It would have been a lot simpler if I'd gone to Barry's as he has the biggest selection I've ever seen, all proudly displayed on his shelves. Only he thinks he's funny and won't sell me any. A joke that goes back to when I was a kid.

But one day Barry, I'll have my copy of Splosh, if it's the last thing I do!

I have been trying on and off all day to get hold of John but my idiot brother still isn't answering his phone. Fingers crossed that at the first sign of trouble he'll grab Emily and come here. As I've said, I have been trying to drum it in to the both of them for years that when the apocalypse hits, the safest place for them to be is with me.

Got to go, I have a strong feeling that tonight is the night. I know the infection has made it to the UK and reports have zombie activity only 20 miles away. It's more than likely already here.

Update –

Holy shit what a night! No sooner had I got out on the roof, I saw the first rumblings of zombie activity. It wasn't easy to see in the dark and at first I thought it was a couple getting up to a bit of rumpy pumpy in the back of a car but on closer inspection using my telescope, I saw what was really happening.

It looked at first like she was giving her fella oral sex but after a good twenty minutes or so of surveillance I saw her lift her head out of his lap and in her mouth was the shredded remains of a penis.

Let it be known that the first zombie I ever saw was a woman eating a man's dick in the back of a Ford Capri.

Then I saw a car crash straight through the living room window of a house. The owner of the house ran out to the car and confronted the driver. Furious he was, pounding his fists on the car roof and kicking the glass in the driver's door window until it shattered. Now I can only guess what the angry man's next moves would have been because from the broken window, a zombie leant out and chomped into his face, biting hard into his nose whilst clawing at his neck. Give the man some credit he fought back alright, picking up a large shard of broken glass and stabbing the zombie in the neck and face repeatedly. It was beautiful!

With all the excitement and fun I was having watching things develop through my telescope, I almost forget to look closer to home. Then I heard groaning coming from below. It was Paula from next door. She was stood in my garden, slouched over, staggering about jaggedly. She was either drunk or dead. I was hoping for the latter.

"Oi, prick!" I shouted.

She lifted up her head and croaked out a hellish groan, revealing her sunken eyes and thin, greying skin. She was dead alright and I couldn't have been happier.

I quickly strapped porno mags to my arms and legs, grabbed a crow bar and climbed down the rope ladder from my back bedroom window. I have to say, the rope ladder isn't the most sturdy of things. I've got a large metal ladder in the garden, I think I'll use that when I can and save the rope ladder for when John and Emily show up so I can laugh at them struggling.

There I was, face to face with my first zombie and lucky for me it was the moaning old cow from next door.

The moment I had been dreaming about for years was about to come true and it couldn't have been any sweeter. I swung the crowbar into the side of her head and it was a great shot even if I do say so myself. She went down like a sack of shit. Dead after one hit. Did I feel any remorse? Not on your nelly. Whilst I wouldn't kill a human (well, unless they hurt me or my family), a zombie is a completely different story. They are already dead, reanimated with one purpose which is to eat human flesh. The only regret I did have was that I would never see her sunbathing topless again. But what the hell, zombies, yay!

As I stood over my first zombie kill, I heard more groaning coming from the front of the house. Cautiously I made my way towards the noise and was delighted to see Ian, my other pain in the arse neighbour heading towards me. He too had sunken eyes and gaunt features with fresh blood covering his mouth and chest.

Wrapped around my lower right leg was a copy of Posh Totty and inside it I had tucked a sharp fishing knife. Removing it I ran at Ian and stabbed him in the head.

My first two kills and it looks like we are dealing with traditional zombies here. Kill the brain kill the shuffler. And what's more, what an amazing start to the apocalypse I'm having. The first two deaders I encounter just so happen to be the two whose heads I had planned to impale on spikes outside my front door!

I heard a loud thud followed by rustling sounds behind me. I turned around to see that trapped in the overgrown brambles and bushes of my front garden was another zombie. It had fallen over the stone wall and gotten trapped, just as I had hoped would happen.

I walked towards it and took a good look at it's cold, pale face and I noticed it sniff the air in front of me before reaching out, attempting to grab a hold. Was the zombie using smell to locate me? I stepped away from the zombie and watched as it did the same thing. Sniffing the air then shifting its head to face me, gnashing its teeth manically. This is something I hadn't expected. It would appear that zombies can pick up the scent of the living. I would have to do more testing to be sure but if I'm right, I can use this to my advantage. I must tell A.R.S.E. what I've found. Right after I've impaled Paula's and Ian's heads on spikes!

Monday

It's Monday morning and the zombie apocalypse has hit Runcorn. I'm not putting the date in this diary from now on as dates don't matter anymore, not to me anyway. If anything today should be 01/01/01 of the new post-apocalyptic world.

The sun has been up for fifteen minutes and I'm about to head out. I mentioned before that it appears zombies can smell the living well I am now in no doubt that they can. This became clear when I walked out on to Weston Road and a small horde immediately turned to face me, all of them sniffing me out.

I retreated back down the stone steps to my house and waited outside the front door watching, as one by one zombies fell over the wall and down the steps. Those that landed in front of me I bashed in with my crowbar and those that got stuck in thick overgrowth I saved till later, stabbing them with my fishing knife.

It took a while and it wasn't easy going but after an hour or so I was surrounded by dead zombies, probably about fifty I'd say. As I stood there, admiring my destruction, I heard more zombies shuffling along the road only, unlike the others, they ignored me and walked past. I can only think of one reason for this and that is they couldn't smell me. The zombies I had killed must have been hiding my scent which has given me a fantastic idea but first, I need to kill more of the bastards! I will update shortly.

Update –

Fuck me I'm knackered. I've spent the last 2 hours using myself as bait to lure zombies into my back garden so I could kill them. Firstly, I removed a fence panel giving me access to the housing estate behind my house then I went hunting. Now like everyone else on this planet I've never hunted zombies before but I found roaming the streets shouting "Here, zombies zombies, here zombies

zombies," seemed to do the trick. It wasn't easy, as every road I walked down was full of people screaming, running, packing cars, boarding up houses, being eaten by loved ones or killing undead loved ones. There was human scent everywhere so to make myself even more appealing, I stripped off to just my underpants so they could smell more of me. I still had porno mags covering my limbs though and I have now also added a lampshade neck protector to my armour. This did the trick and I was soon leading zombies back to my house like I was leading an apocalyptic conga.

As they walked through my fence one by one I stabbed them in the head. You should see the pile of rotters I've amassed outside, it really is a sight to behold. I think I've killed enough now for me to get working on my fantastic idea. But first I need to take a piss. It's thirsty work all this zombie killing.

Update –

It's now early evening and I have spent the last few hours chopping up zombies and nailing their legs, arms, hands, feet and heads to the exterior of my house. Not only will this hide my smell but it should also put the fear of God into any survivors that might be thinking about breaking in.

One thing I've realised is that my zombie protection suit needs modifying. Porno mags, heavy boots and a lampshade neck protector alone won't cut it. I'll have a think and look through my supplies to see what I can add but I'm thinking metal plates on my boots and a stab proof vest. Maybe some shin pads, oh and a tool belt so I can carry more weaponry. I could also do with some tight jeans, maybe even leggings. It dawned on me whilst I was outside wearing only my undercrackers that clothing can give zombies something to grab hold of. So the tighter the better if you ask me.

Update –

It's dark outside now and what a day it's been. There's still a lot more to do tomorrow, starting with hammering stakes into the ground outside my house. If I point them on a slight angle towards the steps and the wall, any approaching zombies should stumble or fall right into them.

I have just checked in with A.R.S.E. to see how everyone is getting on. Only Sky Watcher responded which is worrying. Where the hell are Trust No One and Believe Nothing?

I told Sky Watcher about my discovery that zombies can sniff out the living and what I have done to secure the house further and she has said she will do the same. I'm glad she's OK. Unlike most people in this world I find her really easy to talk to. Plus she makes my cockles jiggle.

I can hear noises outside; I'll update more after I've been to investigate.

Tuesday

That noise I heard outside, well it was only my brother and niece and they had our Emily's boyfriend, Jonathon, and another bloke with them. A Scouser called Dave that looks like he is the president for the Andrew Ridgeley fan club. John said it had taken them all day to get here and he had to rescue Emily from her school which was full of zombies. I'll have a word with Emily in a bit because I have a feeling she was probably doing just fine on her own and it was John that needed rescuing.

It's a weight off my mind having them both here and Dave seems alright. I'm not sure about his choice of weapon but judging by the blood stains on it he's been putting his giant spoon to good use. Plus, looking at the state of John, I'm convinced Dave is the only reason he's still alive. He smokes a lot of cigarettes though. Now I like the odd smoke myself and I had made sure I had enough supplies to last me a few months but watching how many he can put away, my stock won't last us more than a week. We're going to have to go shopping. I think I'll bring Dave with me, he looks like he can look after himself and it will give me a chance to test my new and improved zombie protection suit.

First things first though, I need to wake John up and show him what I have found at the Pavilions. Whilst everyone had a rest I went back out onto my roof to scout our surroundings. Not too far away from us, is a large sports and social club called The Pavilions. It looks as though they have opened their doors for survivors to take shelter. However, the people in there can't see what I can see and obviously don't know that zombies can smell flesh. Every rotter in the area seems to be heading their way. Poor bastards. Once I've shown John what I have found I can put him to work, hammering stakes in the ground. That's if he doesn't cry off, pretending to have a bad back.

Update –

Our shopping trip was a success. Not only did we come back with enough cigarettes to keep Dave happy for a few weeks but we also managed to retrieve more food supplies and alcohol. The alcohol I'm pleased with as it means I don't have to share the homebrew I've got in the cellar. There'll be no cheese beer left if Dave gets a whiff of it; he looks like he's got a thirst on him.

It was also a successful first outing for my new zombie survival suit. I had everything but skinny jeans but luckily Jonathon let me squeeze into his for the mission. I had a bit of fun spinning a yarn to our John that I pinched them from Jonathon whilst he was snuggled up in bed with Emily. You should have seen the look on his face. I think winding my little brother up will be my new hobby.

Dave and I did come into what could have been a problematic situation but we've decided to not tell John and the others. There's no point in worrying them and it's all taken care of now anyway but whilst we were out, we came across some survivors. They were looting the shop we had planned to do ourselves. Outside of the shop was a large transit van filled with food, cigarettes and drink. What's more, it appeared to be unmanned, the looters still inside the shop. Or so we thought!

As we approached the van, a man jumped out and tried to attack us but the bell end tripped and smacked the back of his head on the road. We thought he was dead or at the very least knocked out cold, so we took as much as we could, filled the Thunderbird and scarpered. We were long gone before the survivors in the shop had even realised we were there.

I'm signing off for the night to enjoy food and a few drinks with my family and Dave and Jonathon. Normally I don't take to strangers very well but Dave, despite his bad taste in music and clothes and aside from all the piss taking, is actually an alright bloke. Emily has brought Jonathon round to the house a few times already so I have already gotten to know the kid and I like him a lot. He reminds me of me when I was his age, only I was better looking. He's going to be a good asset to our team, once he learns to curb his enthusiasm a bit. Plus, he's great for our Emily.

Wednesday

Everything has gone to shit. Everything I've been building here has gone and Jonathon… Jesus Christ that poor kid.

Last night, whilst we were sleeping off a good meal and a few beers, my house was set on fire. We were lucky to all escape with our lives or I thought we were. It wasn't till we gathered on the road that we noticed Jonathon wasn't with us. Then the lights from the transit van Dave and I encountered lit up Weston Road and revealed that next to it, Jonathon was tied to a lamp post. The leader shouted to us, something about an eye for an eye and he held up the severed head of the man that jumped out of the van and attacked Dave and I. The bastard thought we'd killed him! Then he set two zombies on Jonathon and drove away.

Two days of things going well and now everything is lost. I can't let the others know how I'm feeling, they expect me to have all the answers. I need to come up with a plan and quickly. The one good thing is that Barry from down the road has taken us in and he is letting us get some rest in his shop. This will give me a little time to think.

Update –

We need to rebuild. Find somewhere we can start again and rebuild, of that there is no question. We also need to make the prick that killed Jonathon and burnt down my home suffer for what he did. How? I'm not so sure at the moment but we need to do something. First things first though, I've told the others we should go back to the house and see if anything can be salvaged. Emily, has barely spoken a word since last night but I can see the rage building inside her. It's within me too. Thankfully, exhaustion has sent her to sleep; she can stay here with Barry whilst the rest of us track back to my house. If the worst comes to the worst and all my supplies have burnt down with the house, then all is not lost. I have more supplies buried in the back garden, we'll just have to move the mountain of zombies to get to them first. I have a little surprise for Dave too. He's been like a different person since the fire melted his Walkman and he lost his Battle Paddle, it's like he's lost his identity. But as I said I have supplies buried in the garden. In fact, I have supplies buried to cater for every apocalyptic scenario imaginable and stored in my robot uprising stash, is a cassette Walkman. That should put a smile on his retro face.

Right, we're off back to what remains of my house. I'll update again later.

Update –

Emily has vanished. No doubt to find the shit that killed Jonathon. John is beside himself, saying it's his fault for leaving her with Barry. I have every confidence that we'll find her. She knows as much as we do and that is that the van from last night drove into Weston Point, so that's where she'll be going and it's where we'll be heading too. Just as soon as we find some transport.

Update –

Still no sign of Emily but we have acquired another addition to our merry band of survivors. Steven his name is and by all accounts he's a bit of a mess. He's mostly slept since we found him standing in the road and if it had been up to me, that's where we would have left him. But John and Dave are soft touches so now we have another misfit amongst our ranks.

Steven told us about a small group of men that murdered his friends and that they were driving a large transit van. It has to be the same people we're looking for. Steven wants revenge also. Maybe he isn't as much of a misfit as I had first thought.

Talking of misfits, we are currently taking shelter in a house and the owner is an agoraphobic traveller called Brittain! Only in Runcorn does this shit happen. He's currently in his kitchen having a drink with Dave who is trying to cure him of his phobia. I'm keeping look out whilst Steven sleeps off his concussion and John is moaning on the couch that it's too noisy to sleep. Maybe I should tell him about the 5 minute power nap experiment and have some fun watching him slowly lose his marbles? I'll think on it for a bit.

The sun should be up in a few hours then we will be on the move again. If Emily has remembered what I've been telling her for years about apocalypse survival, she too will be taking shelter and will also be on the move at first light. She can't be too far away.

Thursday

Another mental day in Zombie infested Runcorn. I am currently sat in an old ladies apartment catching my breath before I have to head out again. We've found the fucker and I have a plan to make him pay. I'll recap all the crazy shit from this morning and bring you up to date whilst I've got a few minutes.

It would appear that Dr Dave, the apocalyptic psychiatrist did the impossible and managed to convince Brittain, who has never stepped foot outside his front door, to go outside. I was sat in the window looking out for zombies and watching the sun come up when I heard the front door open and the young lad stepped outside, albeit gingerly but with a huge smile on his face. I didn't think much of it at first as I was more concerned with us getting back on the road so I didn't mention it to the others. I wish I had done now because by the time I remembered to tell John and Dave, we ran to the door just in time to see a zombie take a huge bite out of him. Poor bastard. How unlucky can you be that the only time you go outside in your entire life you end up getting bit by a zombie? So I did the right thing and ended his life before he turned. The kid had, albeit reluctantly at first, let us stay at his place for the night; we owed it to him not to let him become the undead. See, I do have a heart.

As I wrenched the crowbar out of his mashed up, skull cracked, bloodied, brain oozing head, we heard a loud scraping noise coming from down the road. Then we saw Dave's Thunderbird struggle past, followed by a shit load of zombies. There was a chance it could be Emily, we had to follow it. Plus Dave was beside himself that someone was destroying his beloved car by driving it on four punctured tyres.

We followed the Thunderbird through Weston Point, keeping a safe distance behind the zombies when suddenly the car stopped and hundreds of rotters crowded around it. Well there was only one thing we could do. Drive into as many of the bastards as we could and take them out! As we prepared to ram the fuckers a little red Mini zoomed passed and ploughed into them. Then it reversed back and did it again. I was struggling to see who was driving it and from what I could make out it looked like a cross between Supergirl, a Klingon and The Incredible Hulk! Then she pulled up beside us and asked when we were going to join in!

So we all drove forward and slammed into the horde. As I had feared, Dave's Volvo wasn't up to the task and both he and Steven had to climb out of the window and on to the top of the car. They held the zombies off for a short while but there was just too many of them. Dave managed to jump onto my Land Rover and get inside but Steven didn't make it. We had to watch whilst he was ripped apart by the horde.

With the help of the Hulk fisted girl we continued to ram into the dead until numbers were low enough for us to attack on foot.

It was hard work killing them all but with John, Dave and the girl with the cape, who appeared to be using a sword and a Klingon Bat'Leth, we did it. And when the blood settled and the dead carpeted the road, there she was, our Emily. She was surrounded by dead zombies whilst holding a bloodied hammer. I knew she'd be ok!

Driving the Thunderbird was a fella, Nick he said his name is and with him were a young girl and a baby. He said he had come looking for me because Trust No One told him that when the shit hit the fan, I would know what to do. Unfortunately, Trust No One didn't make it. If only the stubborn old sod had listened to me and not stayed put. Actually, even if he had made it to my place he'd probably be dead anyway. Jonathon, Steven, Brittain, everyone we meet seems to end up dead and now Nick and these kids had turned up. I really didn't want them with us for any longer than they had to be.

Emily took Nick and the kids into an apartment she had been hiding out in whilst Dave, John and I discussed our next move. Then two motorbikes and that transit van we had been looking for appeared, pulling out of the grounds of the Pavilions. We dove for cover, hiding in plain sight amongst the dead zombies. I'm not sure what my brother was playing at but he'd jumped right on top of female zombie. The saucy devil!

Anyway, as it turns out, not only had we found Emily but we had located the prick that killed Jonathon; he was hiding out in The Pavilions. What's more we now have a name for the bastard. Ged he's called and he's teamed up with a bunch of crazies we had encountered yesterday.

With the revelation that the bastard we had been searching for was just around the corner, the girl with the cape that enjoys killing zombies more than I do, disappeared. As quickly as she had turned up she was gone again.

Hopefully we will bump into each other again soon. I've said a few times that adding people to our group isn't a good idea but she is one person whose skills would be an asset to anyone.

Now we knew where he was, we needed a plan to flush him and with the fields surrounding the Pavilions coated in dead zombies, my first thought was to cover ourselves in zombie splodge so that we could pass as rotters, sneak up on him then take him out. John had a moan though and Dave said he would but there was no way he was ruining his clothes. Ruin his clothes? He looks like he's just stepped out of a Dexys Midnight Runners video as it is. Some blood and guts would be an improvement if you asked me.

I do have another plan but I'll have to head down to Mersey road and find a bigger vehicle, maybe a large van or a bus. There's no way I'll get enough ducks up here otherwise.

Also, I need to take Nick and the kids somewhere safe. Enough people have died in our company these last few days, I'm not about to put anyone else at risk. Sky Watcher has said she'll take them in and then, once we have taken care of Ged, we have a place to go to.

I don't know what I'm more nervous about, herding zombie ducks or meeting Sky Watcher for the first time!

Time to move, fingers crossed everything goes to plan.

Update –

Well fuck my hat! We did it! Ged got what was coming to him and Runcorn is a slightly safer place now that the sick bastard and his murderous cronies have been taken care of. My plan worked and with a little help from an ex-employee of Ged's we got him; setting dozens of flesh hungry ducks loose to kill the prick. I got there just in time too as he had found our John and Emily. I hate to think what might have happened if I hadn't turned up when I did.

But it's all over now and we can start the long process of rebuilding, here with Sky Watcher.

I couldn't believe my eyes when I saw her. Dressed head to toe in tight clothing, hard hat, heavy boots and porno mags strapped to her limbs she was a vision of beauty. She was everything I had ever hoped she'd be and more. What's more, she likes me! Normally when I talk to girls they run for the hills screaming or tell the police they think I've escaped from a mental institution but not Sky Watcher.

I think she's the one!

Sky Watcher has done a great job securing her home. Following my instructions she has set traps and nailed zombie limbs to the house too. She lives in a small cul-de-sac next to a large water tower and she is the only survivor left in the street.

Starting tomorrow everything is going to change for us. We have a lot to do but I strongly believe we can secure this street and make it a safe place for us to live. Me and Sky Watcher are going to spend the night drawing up plans whilst the others get some rest, John and Emily in particular. Emily is strong but she has been through a lot these last few days and my brother, well. For a man that jumps at his own shadow and nearly pukes at the thought of mayonnaise, I have to say he's come a long way. Not that I would ever tell him to his face but I'm proud of him. He deserves a little down time.

So tonight, everyone rests so that tomorrow we can get to work building our future.

Building Apocalypse Street.

Printed in Great Britain
by Amazon